Shelley Rivers is a Bournemouth girl who spent most of her childhood reading. Married with a family, she now splits her time between reading, writing, and pandering to the whims of her hilarious greyhound. Her hobbies include lopsided sewing, holey knitting, and collecting old stuff that no one else sees the beauty in.

Also by Shelley Rivers

Tempted by the Brooding Vet

Discover more at millsandboon.co.uk.

AWAKENING
HIS SHY VET

SHELLEY RIVERS

MILLS & BOON

First published in Great Britain 2021
by Mills & Boon, an imprint of HarperCollins*Publishers* Ltd,
1 London Bridge Street, London, SE1 9GF

www.harpercollins.co.uk

HarperCollins*Publishers*
1st Floor, Watermarque Building,
Ringsend Road, Dublin 4, Ireland

Large Print edition 2021

Awakening His Shy Vet © 2021 Shelley Rivers

ISBN: 978-0-263-28792-9

07/21

MIX
Paper from
responsible sources
FSC C007454

Printed and bound in Great Britain
by CPI Group (UK) Ltd, Croydon, CR0 4YY

For Mum—
thank you for always encouraging
the weirdness and the love of colour.

CHAPTER ONE

THE SMELL OF steak pie and the repeat firing of a machine gun made no sense to Ruby Day as she dragged open her heavy eyelids. The long drive from Cambridge to Dorset the previous night had left her exhausted and desperate for nothing but indulging in a further twenty-four hours' worth of sleep.

Frowning at the hot breath fanning her suspiciously damp cheek, she focused blearily on the snoring grey Irish Wolfhound stretched out alongside her, hogging a good portion of the already space-challenged double bed. A slobbering pink tongue hung from his mouth only inches from her nose.

'Dog,' she growled softly. 'When are you going to accept that this is *my* bed, not *yours?* I spent a small fortune on *your* bed—the least you can do is sleep on it occasionally.'

She wiped her cheek, wincing as hound saliva dampened her fingertips. Lovely. What every girl yearned for—doggy dribble for face cream. As if waking to the meaty aroma of canine breath wasn't enough.

Sitting up, she reached for the blue dressing gown draped across the foot of the bed, jumping when loud banging suddenly vibrated through the caravan. Well, that explained the strange machine gun noise in her dream. Not a weapon of destruction, but someone knocking impatiently on the door of her home.

Pushing the still snoring long-legged dog to one side, Ruby slipped out from beneath the warm cover, gasping as her feet hit the cold black-and-white vinyl floor. Tiptoeing to the open bedroom door, she hesitated for a moment, hoping the person knocking would give up and leave. Conversation was the last thing she wanted before caffeine perked the sluggishness from her veins and settled her nerves.

'Hello?' a female voice called out, shattering Ruby's hopes, before another round of banging resumed.

Whoever the woman was, she meant to get a reply, and Ruby doubted even the sinful dead charcoaling in hell would be able to ignore the noise.

'Hi, it's Kiki Morsi. I was wondering if you'd like a cup of tea?'

Ruby stared at the door and a kaleidoscope of thoughts kicked her heart into a galloping trot. Wasn't the man she was here to have an interview with named Morsi? Was this woman his wife? Sister? Mother? Someone related to the man, anyway, and not someone she could just ignore.

Slowly creeping into the kitchen, Ruby eased over to the window by the kitchen sink, grateful that she'd lowered all the blinds the previous night. She'd learnt the hard way to guard her privacy over the years, when closing out the world had become a daily habit.

Leaning over the sink, Ruby felt the metal edge dig through the thin layer of her cotton pyjamas and into her stomach. She peeked through the small crack where the blind didn't quite cover the window frame and got her first sight of her early-morning caller.

A small blonde woman wearing a green coat and a blue woolly hat topped with several multi-coloured pompoms stood in the veterinary practice's car park. She cuddled a tortoiseshell cat against her chest, and an Old

English Sheepdog sniffed intently at her left coat pocket. Apart from the hat, the cat and the dog, she appeared relatively normal.

'Are you Mr Morsi's wife?' Ruby yelled out, grimacing seconds later at the stupidity of her query.

How dumb did she sound, yelling through a closed door with a question a ten-year-old would cringe at? And it didn't matter who the woman was because she needed to go away— and fast.

The woman chuckled and glanced towards the window. 'I am. Can I come in? I promise I'm friendly. It's my husband who's known to growl and occasionally bite.'

Ruby pulled back, her fingers digging into the sink's sides. No way was she opening the door while she stood there in her Christmas reindeer pyjamas without a lick of make-up covering her skin. She never allowed *anyone* to see her without her face on. Not since her sixteenth birthday, when—

She shuffled away, wrapping her arms around her body, suddenly cold from the memory and the lack of heat in the caravan. *No, don't think about it.* It never helped, and her nerves were already rattled over the upcoming interview without adding painful recollections from her past.

'No!' She winced at her bluntness, her nails digging into her elbows.

How to make friends, Ruby. Just keep insulting them and that should get you hated by even more people.

She sucked in a shaky breath, closed her eyes and tried again, 'What I mean is, I—'

Ruby cursed silently. The woman would think her rude, whatever excuse she used, but too bad. She glared towards the bedroom at Dog, who lay content in the middle of her bed, showing a definite lack of the guard dog gene.

'Wh-what I mean is,' she stammered loudly, 'I'm not dressed and the place is a mess. I'll throw on some clothes and be out in ten…no… maybe twenty minutes.'

A pause followed, before the woman outside chuckled. 'Great. Come and join us in Reception when you're ready. Can't wait to meet you, Ruby. Alex is excited too. And ignore my joke about him being growly. He's a real sweet-heart—honest!'

Letting out a sigh of relief at the sound of the woman's retreating footsteps, Ruby slumped against the cupboard. What had happened to her alarm? She remembered setting it last night, after she'd driven into the car park. Alex Morsi had said she could pitch up here in his email, and after travelling for hours the last thing she'd felt like doing was searching for a cara-van park. Most would be fully booked at this time of year anyway, with the schools about to break for the Easter holidays.

She straightened and headed for the bedroom, stepping on the crushed and mangled plastic remains of what used to be her alarm clock, scattered all over her bedroom floor. It was a miracle she hadn't stepped on anything when she'd left the bedroom. Thankfully, the battery showed no signs of canine destruction.

Picking up the pieces, Ruby threw them into the wastepaper bin and glared at the sleep-ing dog. 'I buy you a ton of toys and you eat my alarm clock on the one day I really need it to wake me. Are you trying to make my life harder, Dog? Do you not want me to find a job so we can settle in one place for a while?'

She smiled ruefully at the dog and shook her head.

'You lie there, big boy. Let's hope I can save this cluster of a mess and get through the interview without things getting any worse.'

Tugging a hand through the tangles of the black curly hair that hung in tight ringlets to her shoulders, she headed to the kitchen and retrieved a can of pre-made coffee from a cupboard. Pulling off the lid, she took a long swig, before moving to the small bathroom at the caravan's opposite end.

Once washed and freshened, Ruby snatched up her make-up bag and a magnifying mirror from the shelving unit behind the door. Life in a caravan had taken some getting used to, but now Ruby loved it. When she got bored with a place, or things didn't turn out great, she just packed up and left. No ties, no problems and no trouble.

Returning to the kitchen, she placed the make-up bag and mirror on the table and sat down on the padded seat. Unzipping the bag, she placed its contents carefully on the table, setting each item out in the order she intended to use them.

Picking up a small pot of concealer, two shades lighter than her own natural skin tone, she quickly and expertly sponged the cream over her face and along the length of her neck, taking extra time to camouflage the pink scarring that ran from underneath her jaw and finished just shy of her collarbone.

Once happy the scar no longer showed, Ruby applied powder in a matching colour to set the concealer. Next, she reached for black eyeliner, and with careful, expert strokes swiped a long thick line along the edge of her eyes, ending with an upward tilt at each corner.

Her fingers hovered for several moments over the various different eyeshadows in colours ranging from dark plum to golden-brown. Finally, she chose and applied a shimmering metallic blue shade. A generous brush of thick black mascara finished her eyes perfectly.

Fluttering her eyelashes, she stared at her reflection for a second before reaching for a blue lipstick. Several slick swipes and her eyes and lips matched. A clean cotton bud wiped superfluous lipstick from the silver ring in the centre of her lower lip.

With a final spray of face mist to set the make-up in place, she took one last glance in the mirror. Transformation completed and armour on. Now she could face the next hour and the upcoming interview.

'Hello, Ruby Day. Time to face the world again.'

She studied her reflection for a moment longer, taking in the black curly hair and the pale skin hiding the scar. Eyes large and dramatic… lips full and plump. A face to show to a cold and uncaring public who loved to revel in other people's misery with morbid interest. The perfect face to hide behind in a world that chose to see only the make-up and not to search further to learn who the woman was underneath.

That suited Ruby. With this make-up nobody instantly recognised her mother's model face in hers. No one compared her to her parent or asked about the father she'd supposedly betrayed. With this make-up people didn't gaze at her with pity, interest or horror.

At sixteen years old, her teenage self had learnt several hard lessons, and one was how to create a defence against the hurt and pain others wanted to inflict on her. Over time her make-up and clothes had become her secure shield.

She turned the mirror upside down, hiding her reflection from view, and stood. She walked into the bedroom and changed into a pair of tight black jeans and a black T-shirt with a large silver cross on the front. After adding several silver bracelets and a necklace with a large silver and blue heart dangling from it, she finally tugged on black leather boots.

If her make-up didn't send Alex Morsi into convulsions, her clothes definitely would.

She finished the outfit off with a fitted vintage black velvet jacket that had once belonged to her mother. She stroked a hand over the soft, smooth material—it was one of the few items she'd kept from the past, and a connection to the woman she loved and missed every day.

With a final quick check in the full-length mirror attached to the back of the bedroom door, she grabbed her black leather handbag and left the room.

Alex Morsi and his staff would no doubt be like all the other practices she'd applied to.

Ready to dismiss her application the minute they set eyes on her. After all, who employed someone who dressed with an unmistakable Goth vibe? No one who owned a veterinary practice, that was for sure.

This whole trip to Dorset was nothing but a waste of time and petrol money. Why she had promised her old tutor, Professor Handel, to give it one last go, she didn't know. Misplaced gratitude, probably. The woman had frequently gone out of her way to help Ruby during the years she'd studied at college, becoming more than a tutor—she'd become a real friend.

Ruby already dreaded the evening phone call she'd promised to make, when she'd have to confess that, yet again, she'd not secured the position. Though for some reason, Professor Handel had insisted that Alex Morsi was different.

Yeah, right. No doubt Morsi was another middle-aged vet who wore tweed and fashioned himself on the old television dramas so often repeated on TV.

She was tired of it all. Not just driving miles to each interview, but the horrified expressions that greeted her appearance and the hastily concocted excuses and promises to call back— calls she never received. So what if she dressed differently and liked dramatic make-up? Her clothes made her feel safe and able to face the world.

No one complained or looked strangely at ordinarily dressed candidates when they turned up for an interview.

But no more, Ruby decided, snatching up a bunch of keys from the kitchen table. The events of the past had left her with no choice but to dress and look this way. After this interview she was done trying. Time to finally face reality and pack away the dream of becoming a practising vet for good.

Kern MacKinley lay on the grass, staring up at the sky, almost gagging on the bitter taste of failure. Memories old and painful gnawed and tore at his conscience, burning reminders of a past he'd done his damnedest to bury and forget.

Nineteen years he'd stayed away from this farm. Nineteen long, exciting years filled with the heady, sweet taste of ambition and success. Nineteen years of hard work and determination, during which everything he'd hoped and dreamed of professionally had come true. Wonderful, perfect days, weeks and months filled with glory and triumph as he clawed, climbed and fought to build his reputation as one of the top racehorse trainers in the country—if not the world.

He was a man people admired and looked up to. Someone whose work ethic and training methods they respected and revered.

But now he lay on the Dorset land of his childhood and everything he'd built and achieved during those heady nineteen years sat in failure and decay. Ruined beyond hope or fixing. Thirty-eight years old and he had nothing left in his life but regret and heartbreak after all those years battling to be one of the best in horse racing.

Now he was nothing more than a lousy failure!

The only thing that had survived the bloody carnage was now so broken it might have been kinder if she'd died with the rest. Then at least her pain and sorrow wouldn't be trapped inside her, like a festering wound waiting to explode.

Rubbing a hand over the ache in his chest, he

sighed, his eyes following a cloud as it floated above him. There was no one to blame for the whole horrendous mess but his own sweet self. He'd purposely stuck his pig-stubborn head in the ground and pretended not to see the problems stewing in his personal life—or listen to the one person who mattered.

And what had his obstinacy cost him?

Everything.

His reputation, three prized racehorses who'd deserved his protection, and the woman he'd once upon a time promised to love and treasure. The woman who, despite the problems in their relationship, had deserved his help when it might have made a difference. Before it had all finally been amplified into the catastrophe it had become.

Closing his eyes, he refused to picture her face, burying the image in the murky pit of denial. Even now, after everything, it was still a habit he found himself unable to break. Better to hold back than confront the unpleasant facts of what his selfishness had driven another person to do.

Opening his eyes, he forced his mind to the present. All he owned sat in two cardboard boxes on the passenger seat of the old horsebox parked not far away, together with one emotionally damaged horse, five thousand pounds in his pocket, an old inheritance he didn't want and a throbbing hangover courtesy of the bottle of vodka that had kept him company last night.

His life was well and truly stuffed.

Ignoring the pressing discomfort of a full bladder, he continued to stare unseeingly at the sky. What the hell was he supposed to do now? Two days ago he'd come back to Dorset so his wife's ashes could finally be scattered in her family's special spot, and he'd stayed.

Where did a has-been go when the world turned away, determined and eager to forget him?

The recent months had left him with no choice but to sell everything he'd worked for, to pay his debts and walk away. Forcing him to accept charity and hand-outs from people he'd never considered friends, while the ones he'd thought were had deserted him without even a goodbye.

Out of habit, he reached for his mobile, resting in the centre of his bare chest, and checked for messages. His thumb slipped over the screen in pathetic hope. Hope that quickly died after several seconds. Nothing except a message from his service provider, notifying him that he needed credit.

No one called any more. These days his phone stayed silent because his name was shrouded in whispers, gossip and scandal. He was someone no sane person in the racing world wanted to trust with the care of their precious thoroughbred livestock. A trainer no one wanted to touch. The last nineteen years had all been for nothing.

What the hell was he going to do now?

Everything was wrecked because he hadn't seen the damage that chasing after his dreams had caused to the one person he should have protected and helped.

God, what an idiot he was.

A noise drew his attention back to the sky. Three white gulls flew above him, squawking as they went. Their large wings flapped in perfect timing as they headed some place new.

A rare smile tugged at Kern's lips. 'Have a safe journey—'

Suddenly something swooped over him. A

second later a small red and brown robin landed on his bare stomach.

'Well, hello,' he whispered, not wanting to scare the bird.

Small dark eyes stared back, before the robin started pecking at the wiry hairs circling Kern's tummy button.

'Ouch! No. That's attached, you little—'

Kern registered something wet and warm on his skin a second after the robin flew off. Glancing down, he saw bird droppings splattered across his stomach.

Great, even the wildlife wanted to echo how crap his life was.

'Thanks!' he yelled to the long-gone bird. 'Like I need the reminder.'

Rolling onto his feet, Kern stared at the river that marked the edge of MacKinley land. Dressed in nothing but blue boxers, he strolled towards it, feeling the damp grass cushioning his footsteps, the green blades tickling his toes.

It was the same river where he'd played and swum during his childhood. He'd kissed his first sweetheart and eagerly tried to lose his virginity behind the bushes that grew in places along the bank. It was where he'd thought up boyhood daydreams and big plans. Back when his mother had run the place and kept his step-father out of Kern's business.

A time before she'd betrayed him and everything he'd once thought true. Long before he'd fallen in love with a neighbour's youngest daughter and run away with her. Before he'd married her and formed a new life away from their families. A time before he'd bought his first racehorse and won his first major trophy.

Coming to a halt on the bank, he dug his toes into the grass and breathed in a lungful of sharp morning air. Wriggling the gold wedding ring off his finger, he glanced at it for several long seconds, sad that its familiar sight no longer stirred any emotions. Was he so far gone now that she'd ripped even that from him? Killed the last threads of his affection so that the act of removing this ring for the first time in nineteen years left him feeling nothing?

Drawing his arm back, he threw the ring into the air, watching as it flew, then dropped, breaking through the water's surface with a loud, distinct *plop.*

Now that last connection was gone too. Relegated to nothing but a memory to shovel on to the huge pile of disappointment his life had become.

He'd returned to this old run-down farm because there was no other place to go.

With that final thought, he jumped into the freezing water, gasping as it swirled over his skin and froze every inch of his body.

Scrambling back out of the water, his fingers grasping at the mud and grass, he crawled onto the bank with all the style and finesse of a flapping, gaping fish. Bent over on all fours, he dragged air into his shocked lungs as his mind vaguely registered the loss of feeling in his body.

How the hell had he forgotten how cold the river was? His life was already on the slide, without adding the agony of self-inflicted frozen body parts too.

They were staring. After years of enduring similar behaviour from strangers, Ruby had expected it and now fought the urge to stick out her tongue. Every time she arrived somewhere new the stares began, triggering prickles of tension as she prepared for the remarks and insults that followed. The nosy, ridiculous questions that always ended up becoming too personal.

She pretended not to notice as she stepped into the reception area. Closing the door, she caught the faint smell of disinfectant in the air, mixed with the whiff of rich coffee. Two women stood behind the counter. One she recognised as Kiki Morsi—the other was a grey-haired older woman.

'Ruby?' With a smile, Kiki stepped from behind the counter and walked over to greet her. Dressed in blue animal print scrubs, she held out a hand in welcome. 'It's lovely to meet you. I hope you didn't mind my knocking earlier? Only I've been so looking forward to your arrival.'

Not sure what to say, Ruby shook Kiki's hand, conscious of the intense gaze of the woman at the counter.

'My husband's finishing some paperwork and other important chores he apparently has to see to,' Kiki continued. 'I suspect they involve cuddling and singing to our daughter. Come and meet Anne.'

The woman behind the counter leaned forward. Her smile was wide and genuine. 'Nice to meet you, Ruby. Is your hair naturally curly, or thanks to chemicals and a skilled hairdresser?'

Stunned, Ruby stared at the woman before answering. Of all the things she'd expected, comments on her hair wasn't one of them. 'It's natural.'

'It's very pretty,' Kiki agreed, tilting her head to one side. 'Much better than my boring straight blonde mop. I'm going bald, you know—'

'You've just had a baby,' Anne interrupted. 'I keep telling you it will grow back. It's your messed-up hormones.'

'That's what Alex dared to say the last time we disagreed.' Kiki sighed. 'Until I threatened to stick his expert opinion somewhere uncomfortable. Anyway, enough about me and the love of my life. Tell me all about yourself, Ruby.'

'Ignore her, dear,' Anne said. 'She's recently returned from maternity leave and she's trying to get her fix of female conversation and gossip before she starts work for the day.'

Kiki grinned and nodded. 'All true. Though she forgot to mention that I'm incredibly nosy, too.'

Ruby laughed, envying the women's easy camaraderie. Their chattiness was something she wasn't used to and had never experienced for herself. Normally people avoided talking to her or just stared.

'So you live in that box, do you?' Anne asked, pointing out of the large window to Ruby's caravan.

Ruby stiffened, waiting for further remarks about her unusual home. Okay, it might not be everyone's idea of home, but she loved it. It was her sanctuary. Her place to escape when she required a private moment alone. Her 'Ruby' space, where she could lower her walls, wash off her make-up and be her true self.

'Yes.'

Anne shivered and folded her arms on the counter. 'Must get cold in the winter. It would play my old bones up something awful.'

It did get cold, but Ruby refused to admit it and felt a silly need to defend her home take hold. 'Actually, it's quite cosy.'

The sound of someone clearing his throat stopped further conversation.

Ruby turned to find a tall, dark-haired man frowning at the blonde woman at her side. His serious expression was a sharp contrast with the pink baby carrier strapped to his waist, holding a wriggling and softly grunting child.

His eyes flicked to Ruby, lingered for a second before returning to Kiki. 'Our daughter needs feeding.'

Kiki smiled, her expression softening as she gazed at the man and child. 'Stop frowning—you'll scare Ruby away. I'll get Neeve's bottle for you. Be *nice*.'

The man grunted, then returned his full attention to Ruby. His eyes narrowed for several seconds, before he held out his hand. 'Miss Day?'

Seized by nerves, Ruby grappled for her courage before placing her hand in his. She tried to speak, but her voice wouldn't work.

Not the tweed-wearing country vet she'd imagined, but although he was good-looking and young, Alex Morsi still gave off an unapproachable air that told her she didn't have any hope of getting a job at his practice. No doubt he was already figuring out a way to get rid of her and save himself the inconvenience of having to go through with the interview.

'I'm Alex Morsi.' He rubbed a loving hand over the baby's back, glancing to the older woman behind the desk. 'Anne, have you sent anyone to MacKinley farm yet?'

'Nope. Eloise said her nephew wanted you to go.'

Alex frowned and shook his head. 'I'm too busy with Neeve.' He glanced once again in Ruby's direction. 'Miss Day can go. From what I've read and heard, horses are her passion and her area of expertise.'

Kiki returned, carrying a bottle of baby's milk and a cloth. She handed both to her husband with a frown. 'Her name's Ruby, Alex.'

'I know,' Alex murmured, taking the bottle and throwing the cloth over his shoulder. 'Your CV states that you have a strong interest in equine health and have volunteered at several horse rescue centres in order to work with a couple of top specialists. Professor Handel also mentioned your gift.'

Ruby stiffened, unsure how to answer. How much had her old professor divulged about her supposed 'gift'? Neither of them had made it public knowledge during her training. Why had her mentor and friend trusted this man with the information?

Forcing herself to meet Alex's eyes, Ruby

found only curiosity in his gaze. Deciding it might be best to blag her way through the rest of the conversation, while she tried to gauge how much he actually knew, she nodded. 'Yes, I loved helping out and I found the work fascinating.'

'Good. I'd like to observe you in action some time.'

Ruby didn't know what to say, so she stayed quiet. Should she trust his apparent interest or not? Did he want to watch her so he could afterwards pooh-pooh her gift as nothing but a charlatan's work? Surely Professor Handel should have warned her that she had told Alex Morsi about it.

Alex nodded, taking her silence as agreement. 'So you're the best person to deal with this visit, Miss Day. Anne will give you directions to the farm. No point relying on satnav— it's useless out there.'

Confused, Ruby asked, 'You want me to go and see a horse?'

Alex nodded. 'Yes. The owner wants a general check done. Nothing you can't manage. His name is Kern MacKinley. Have you heard of him?'

She shook her head. 'No.'

'He's a racehorse trainer,' Anne piped up. 'Damn good one too. Never met him, so I have no idea what he's like to deal with, but he's in the area and he wants his horse looked over. It isn't a good traveller or something. Nothing major or concerning, but best you go out and put the man's mind at ease.'

'Okay...'

'Don't worry, dear,' Anne said, writing something in a notebook. 'You'll be fine. I don't know Kern MacKinley—do know his aunt, though. Wonderful woman. Blunt to the point of rudeness, but honest to deal with. I've seen the nephew on television, of course. Handsome man...if you like them rough and smelling of horses. Avoid the stepfather if he's about. My Harry gets on with him well enough, but I've no time for the man.'

'I'll pop your tea in a flask, shall I?' Kiki asked brightly. 'You can take it with you. I think there are a couple of spare chocolate croissants in the kitchen too.'

Ruby frowned as Kiki rushed off again. Was this some bizarre dream?

She turned to Alex and asked, 'But don't you want to interview me?'

He sighed. 'Isn't Professor Handel's endorsement enough? She spoke very highly of you during our phone call the other day.'

'I—I don't know...' she stammered. 'Is it?'

'Miss Day, can you do the job? Are your qualifications real and up to date?'

Pulling herself together before she ruined this chance, Ruby nodded. 'Yes, of course they are.'

'Then off you go. I've no time to waste on interviewing you when my daughter needs feeding. It's best you learn, Miss Day, that my family always comes first. We can chat later, when you return, and go through everything you need to know. Will that please you?'

Ruby's mouth fell open as he walked away, kissing his wife on the head as they passed each other.

'It's Ruby, Alex,' Kiki reminded him brightly.

He snorted. 'I know. Until later, Miss Day.'

Kiki held out a blue flask to Ruby. 'My husband's really sweet when you get used to him. A year or two should do it.'

Confused, Ruby took the flask. 'He did give me a job, didn't he? I have that right?'

'Oh, yes. Trust me—Alex wouldn't let you near a client if he wasn't sure you knew your stuff. I'm sure he quizzed Professor Handel and checked your qualifications thoroughly.' She smiled once more and shoved a plastic bag holding two croissants Ruby's way. 'Welcome to the family, Ruby. It's good to have you here.'

CHAPTER TWO

RUBY SLAMMED ON the brakes and stared at the sight that had greeted her within moments of turning off the country lane and onto MacKinley land. No sooner had she bumped her way over the cattle grid, then bounced over several stomach-tilting potholes, she'd glanced to her left and set eyes on an almost naked man, kneeling on all fours beside a river.

Screwing her eyes shut, Ruby paused, then opened them again, convinced that the vision was nothing more than an illusion of her mind, brought on by the shock of actually securing her dream job and the peculiar way it had happened.

But, no, there the man knelt, in nothing but tight blue boxer shorts, almost as exposed as the beautiful nature in the field surrounding him.

What the heck had Alex Morsi sent her to deal with?

No one at the practice had mentioned anything about the risk of encountering an unclothed male. Was this some test, specially concocted to mess with the newbie vet? Was there even a horse requiring a visit, or was this all some stupid practical joke on her?

Pushing open the car door, Ruby slowly climbed out, unable to move her eyes from the sensual curve and dip of the man's back above the material so snugly covering the round curve of his very firm backside.

She was embarrassed by her own staring, but she couldn't stop herself. Apart from the countryside, and an old horsebox, there wasn't much else to look at. And from this angle the man appeared to be a perfectly formed specimen of masculinity.

Flushing at her thoughts, Ruby reluctantly moved in the man's direction and called out. 'Hello? I'm Ruby Day. Alex Morsi sent me from the vet's practice in town. Are you all right?'

The man glanced up, water dripping down his face. and puffed. 'I will be in a sec. Just waiting for things to defrost.'

'Defrost?'

'Yeah. My blood, for one, and other more sensitive parts of my body. Right now I'm struggling to feel anything from my waist down.'

'Oh,' Ruby said, wondering if he was one of those endurance swimmers who liked to pit themselves against nature.

Getting awkwardly to his feet, the man stared at her for several moments before demanding, 'Is he on his way?'

Good grief. Ruby glanced away, forcing her gaze to a nearby hedge despite the irresistible and unexpected urge to sneak a second eyeful. Anne had said the man was good-looking, but he made even her handsome new boss look plain. Tall, wide-chested and shivering, the man literally made her mouth water.

The man called out again. 'Hey? Miss?'

With no choice but to look at him, she resisted the childish urge to cover her eyes and croaked, 'Yes?'

'I asked if Morsi is on his way,' the man repeated, walking towards her.

His lack of embarrassment over his undressed state and his determination to talk to her while in it was unsettling. How was she supposed to have a conversation with him when he was so blatantly uncovered and when his swim had left the material of his boxers clinging rather rudely to him?

'Are you going to answer me or simply stand there?' he asked.

Ruby squirmed on the spot, unsure whether to shut her eyes or take off and make for the safety of her car.

Heat warming her cheeks, she folded her arms and admitted, 'To be honest, I'm debating whether to cover my eyes or leave.'

'Why?'

Surely the man knew?

She waved a hand towards his lower body. 'I wasn't expecting to arrive and find you so unclothed.'

Silence followed by a sharp intake of breath came from the man, before he glanced down at himself and said. 'God, can things get any worse?'

He spun round and hurried over to the horse-box and dragged on a pair of jeans. Sliding them on and up over his firm wet thighs with difficulty, he zipped them, before returning to Ruby.

'Sorry about that,' he puffed. 'Truth is I forgot I was only wearing my boxers.'

'You *forgot*?' she echoed disbelievingly.

He rubbed a hand over his head and sighed. 'Yes.'

'Really?' she drawled, doubting the truth of his apology. Who forgot they weren't wearing their clothes? The very fact that everything was exposed to the air proved his words a lie. 'Hmm... Do you often go swimming in the river in just your underwear?'

'Not any more,' he muttered. 'Not until summer, at least.'

She wasn't a prude, but she really hadn't expected her first call to involve an undressed male. Glancing at his still bare chest, she noticed water dripping in rivulets down over the well-defined hard muscles to hang like clear jewels from his dusky nipples. Her tongue tingled at the sight.

Her eyes moved farther down, stopping when they came to a strange patch of sludge splattered across his stomach.

'What's that?' she asked, trying to work out what the strangely familiar-looking muck was. It reminded her of watered-down grease, but it also resembled—

'What?' the man asked.

'There.' She pointed at the offending mess. 'On your stomach, just above your jeans.'

He clenched his jaw. 'It's nothing.'

'It looks like bird's m—'

'It's mud.'

'Mud?' she repeated. 'It doesn't look like mud. It's whitish, for one, and the patterning reminds me of—'

'The soil around here has a high chalk content,' he insisted.

She narrowed her eyes and considered the mess again. 'Are you sure? It does look an awful lot like—'

'It's nothing. I'll wash it off later. Now, about Morsi.'

'Don't you have a shirt or jumper?' she asked, deciding to forget about the muck on his stomach and get on with her job. 'Or is your memory so bad you've forgotten where you've put them?'

His eyes narrowed. 'No, I remember fine, thanks.'

'Then please fetch one and put it on. I'd really prefer to speak to you without any unnecessary distractions.'

He grinned, losing his serious expression for

the first time. 'Distraction, huh? I'll take that as a compliment.'

'It's not meant as one,' she bit back, flustered slightly by the sudden roguish twinkle in his blue eyes and the suggestiveness warming his voice.

It was a voice capable of seduction if he chose to use it. Not that she would ever be seduced by it. But she understood some women would find the effect of his deep silky tones coupled with his attractive body irresistible and maybe a bit knee-weakening.

'Well?' he asked, still smiling. 'Is Morsi coming?'

'No,' she said, wondering if he was some kind of exhibitionist.

Did he get a kick out of cavorting half-naked in his field? Well, he could do what he liked in private, but she wanted him covered. Preferably all over! Head to toe—twice over! Finger to finger and everything in between.

'Alex—Mr Morsi—asked me to call instead.'

His humour vanished at her reply. 'But I need someone with experience.'

'I *am* experienced,' she replied, not about to be bullied or intimidated into leaving before she saw her patient. Alex Morsi had given her the chance to prove herself and she wasn't going to fail at the first hurdle—or the first grumpy man with odd tendencies to nakedness and covered in suspected bird droppings.

He folded his arms and regarded her. 'You're a qualified vet? You're very young.'

Ruby closed the space between them. 'Mr MacKinley? I guess you *are* Mr MacKinley? Only you've yet to have the decency to introduce yourself other than to expose yourself in a fashion I would prefer *not* to see you in.'

'You sure?' he asked, his eyes once again flashing with humour.

'Yes, I'm s-sure,' she stuttered, tilting her chin up. 'Mr MacKinley, I am a qualified vet and more than capable of examining your horse. I have a degree to prove it.'

Crossing his arms, he asked, 'Is that supposed to mean something to me?'

'It means that your horse will be treated not only by someone who knows her stuff, but has the documentation to prove it.' She hoped he wouldn't demand to know how much actual experience she'd had, otherwise she would be forced to tell a little white lie.

He hesitated. 'My aunt gave me Morsi's name. Not yours.'

'I'm afraid he's busy,' she said, picturing Alex Morsi with his baby daughter. How would Mr MacKinley react if she informed him that her new boss put feeding his child before every-thing—including this man's precious horse? 'He sent me instead.'

'My girl isn't any old nag. She's a top thor-oughbred.'

'She's a horse, no matter what her bloodline is or how much she's worth, Mr MacKinley. One whom I will be able to treat. If she's sick, I need to examine her.'

'She's not sick,' he hedged. 'I just want some-one to check her over. We've done a lot of trav-elling over the last few days.'

Ruby nodded, not seeing a problem other than a trainer's protectiveness. 'Fine. If you'll show me where she is…?'

He stared back at her, then grinned. 'You blush when you're embarrassed.'

Gritting her teeth, Ruby replied, 'I am not embarrassed—merely shocked by your unorth-odox behaviour. *Annoyed* is a better description of how I'm feeling.'

'You reacted as though you'd never seen a man in only his underwear before,' he persisted, not letting the subject go.

'Your horse, Mr MacKinley?'

Intense blue eyes stared down at her.

'Lady, that horse is all I have left in the world. Only the best vet is going to get anywhere near her.'

'I *am* the best, Mr MacKinley.'

An out-and-out lie, but one day Ruby intended to be. Once she had real everyday experience and a chance to prove herself. Something she was determined to do now that Alex Morsi had given her the opportunity and the means.

Kern MacKinley regarded her for a long moment, then said, 'Then I guess you'd better prove it to me.'

'I intend to, sir,' she replied, but the man had already turned and walked away.

What the hell was Morsi up to? Sending some young woman to do his job? Kern continued to walk in the direction of the back paddock while buttoning his shirt. His mind was still full of the recent exchange between him and the woman trailing several paces behind him.

For such a shy woman, she packed a fair slap-down when roused.

He'd asked for the practice's top vet and they'd sent out Miss Ruby Day, with her weird make-up and her hair so thick and curly his fingers begged to slide into it and discover if it really was as soft and bouncy as it appeared. A woman who'd nearly choked on her prissy tongue when faced with a wet naked chest and more.

Irritated, he pushed the notion away. Miss Vet was no doubt waiting for Mr Right to come along and dance her up the altar. Some man who'd make promises he'd struggle to keep.

Once he'd been that man, to his own Miss Right, little knowing that she'd eventually become his Mrs Wrong, who'd refuse to listen to anything but the poisonous whispers in her head.

He sighed, feeling the weight of everything once again settling heavily on him.

To reach the paddock meant passing the old grey brick farmhouse he'd grown up in. Kern had purposely avoided the building since he'd driven onto the land, but now he had no choice.

Memories of his bedroom up in the thatched

roofed attic swept over him. He'd moved up there after his mother had married her second husband. He glanced up at the small window in the roof. Did the room still hold everything he'd left behind? Did his once-treasured keepsakes still sit on the shelves? Had his posters yellowed and faded?

A part of him ached to go inside and find out. To reach out and touch the past for just a brief moment.

'Who's she?'

The question interrupted Kern's reminiscing. His stepfather was walking out through the front door of the farmhouse towards them. Well, staggering described his movements better. Kern's hangover was nothing but a minor inconvenience compared to the one he suspected bothered the old man.

Great—dealing with Fin was the last thing he needed right now.

'No one,' Kern answered briskly. 'Leave us to our business. It has nothing to do with you.'

'Wrong,' Fin snapped, stumbling closer. He raised a shaky hand and pointed at Kern. 'If you think I'm going to let you turn up and start ordering me around, then you're wrong. Maybe

I need to teach you a lesson, like I did when you were younger.'

Resisting the urge to snap his stepfather's finger, just to stop his ranting, Kern searched and found the last piece of his patience. He wasn't a kid any more, and no matter how low he fell he'd never stoop as low as Fin.

'Forty-five per cent is yours—the rest belongs to me.'

'I'm the one who kept everything going while you swanned around drinking champagne with your fancy crowd. Where are they now, hey? Since your golden crown has fallen off your damn big head? Where are they now, boy?' He cackled. 'Gone. Just like your career. It's the only reason you've come back here to trouble me.'

'Shut up,' Kern warned him, not needing his problems to be shared with the vet. His life's mistakes concerned no one. The woman didn't need to know that failure hung around his neck like an unwanted bridle.

'No one wants to know the great Kern Mac-Kinley now, do they?' Fin continued. 'Your name must really be dirt if the only sort of woman you're attracting is *her* kind.' He glanced at the vet and grimaced. 'A step down for you, boy, isn't she? From all the blondes who used to flutter around you at the race courses. You'd be better off paying for a woman's time than picking up a freak like *her* from the gutter.'

Kern's patience evaporated, and before Fin could utter another insult he grabbed the old man by the shirt. The woman deserved better than bearing Fin's slurs and bitterness.

Temper and frustration pumped through his blood as he faced the man who'd given his mother such a hard time during the last years of her life. 'Shut your damn mouth. There's nothing wrong with her. Got that? She's a queen compared to a nasty old dog like you. At least she doesn't stink of body odour and urine. When was the last time you bathed?'

'Get your hands off me!' Fin cried, all his bravado vanishing beneath Kern's temper. 'Beating up old men impresses her, does it?'

'I wouldn't waste my time.' Kern shoved him away, furious they'd not managed five minutes before they were at each other's throats.

He watched the sour old man turn and head into the farmhouse and slam the door. A black iron horseshoe fell off and hit the stone step with a dull clang. Who knew what state the old place was in after all these years of housing Fin and his addiction?

He glanced at the vet, his heart tugging as he took in her bent head and the way she hugged herself. Clearly a protective stance. How many times had she endured hurtful comments from strangers because she dressed a little differently and wore make-up in unusual colours?

An unexpected urge to comfort her tugged at him, but he buried it, not about to scare the woman further. Although Fin must be blind as well as useless if he couldn't see the beauty in this woman's lines and form. She reminded him of a newly born foal. With long, shapely legs and an unconfident delicacy to her movements.

'Mr MacKinley, are you all right?'

Kern blinked several times as her question penetrated his wandering thoughts. 'I'm sorry about Fin. Ignore his stupidity. My stepfather is a drunk and bitter man. He married my mother expecting to inherit this farm when she died, and turned vicious when he discovered he never would—not completely. It's a family farm and the majority owner will always be a blood relation. Besides, he's an idiot. Any man can see you're a stunner.'

She stared at him as though his words had shocked her. Surely someone—a parent, a boyfriend or a lover—had told her the same? Even an old cynic like him could see that Miss Vet was a beautiful woman.

A deep flush coloured her cheeks beneath her make-up and she glanced towards the paddock. 'Your horse?' she said again.

The sight of her blush pulled at Kern's battered heart and he changed his mind. Folding his arms, he shook his head. 'I think it's best you leave. I'll give the practice a call in a few days if my horse still hasn't settled.'

'But Mr MacKinley...'

'Truth is, Fin will be out here again in a few minutes, once he's drunk some fresh courage. Now's not a good time for you to stay around. Things will get uglier than they already have. I'll call and make another appointment once I'm confident you'll not get caught in the middle of our argument. Okay?'

'But—but...' she stammered.

Kern placed his hands on his hips and sighed.

'I'm sorry—but my property, my rules. I'm afraid it's past time for you to leave, Miss Day.'

What a mess. Kern stared around at the run-down stables, unsure whether to yell until his throat burned or toss a lit match on the whole place and drive north.

Disrepair and neglect stared back at him, no matter where his eyes settled. From the piles of dried manure to the stable doors hanging off rusty hinges.

Paint flaked from walls once adorned from top to bottom with multicoloured rosettes. These derelict stables had once homed some of the best horses in the country. Now they were fit for nothing more than flattening with a bulldozer.

Large cobwebs hung from the sloped beamed ceiling like fragile Halloween decorations, gently moving from side to side thanks to the draughts coming through the roof where there were missing tiles. Thick mould grew in dark corners and heavily scented the air.

Fin had a lot of explaining to do once he sobered up. Not just about the decay of this building, but the rest of the farm.

Kern had taken a walk up to the old gallops his grandfather had created, back in the 1950s, and he'd had to fight his way through thick overgrown bushes and hip-high weeds just to reach the start. The rest of the course wasn't much better.

'It's a sight to hurt the optics and the heart, isn't it?' a familiar female voice remarked behind him.

Though its tones were aged, he would recognise that accent in a crowd of cheering racegoers any day.

Not sure what to expect from the woman, he slowly turned and braced himself to see her for the first time in nineteen long years. 'Eloise…'

Eloise Blake, his aunt, had collected her share of wrinkles and shrunk several inches in height, but he could still see the tough spirit of the woman he'd once known in her hazel eyes and straight back. Even now she stood holding the lead rope of a pretty brown mare.

'*Aunt* Eloise, if you don't mind,' she replied, her displeasure clear in both her voice and gaze. 'I haven't forgiven you yet and I'm not sure I want to.'

Figuring it best to forget polite chit-chat and

face the full wrath of his aunt's anger, he asked, 'Why the hell didn't you tell me how bad Fin had let things get?'

Eloise raised a brown pencilled eyebrow and stared down her straight nose. Her right hand gripped a pink walking stick. 'Would you have cared?'

The question hit him right in the chest, where he suspected she'd meant it to. Never one to pull her punches, his aunt had something on her mind and he might as well let her spit it out if he wanted answers.

He sighed. 'What's that supposed to mean?'

'Let's not kid ourselves, young man,' she said, disappointment in every syllable. 'I'm no fool and you're no liar... Well, you never were. I called Corinne time and again over the years, and every time she insisted you didn't care. That you'd kicked us and this place from your heels without regret. Yet now you stand here complaining. As though this is all my fault. As though I was the one who walked away.'

Confused, Kern asked, 'She did what?'

'She said you'd left us all behind for a reason and that you had far more important things to deal with than this farm.' She lifted the walking stick and pointed it at him. 'Oh, she enjoyed telling me that, you know. Never could keep the glee from her voice when she did it.'

Kern clenched his hands, absorbing this latest discovery of his wife's betrayal. Never had he said anything about not wanting to hear from his aunt. He'd believed it was the other way around, when after the first year he'd heard nothing from his relative despite the fact he had written with his new address and phone number.

'She never told me you called.'

Eloise sniffed and lowered the stick. 'I bet she didn't. Well, I honestly don't suppose it would have made any difference if she had. You never called me either, did you? No, you turned your back on this place and moved on, just as your dear mother predicted you would. Yes, she was right about that.'

Mention of his mother brought fresh irritation. The woman he'd loved and believed loved him. The woman who'd gambled with his inheritance and then left him with the resulting mess when she'd died too young.

'Do you blame me?'

'For leaving?' Eloise shook her head. 'No. I

understood in the beginning. You always had a temper and your mother spoilt you. But I hoped once you'd calmed down and thought about things you would eventually trail home. You didn't—and *that* is what upsets me the most. This place, its history, the people who built it—your own family—you walked away from it all. So, yes, you *are* to blame for the broken roof on the stables and the overgrown, weed-thick paddocks, and the fact that not one horse calls this place home any more. Your mother loved this farm and sacrificed her happiness for it. When she left you her share of the place she did it because she hoped you'd grasp it and make a new history for it. Continue her and your grandparents' legacy. Yet all you've done is prove her greatest fears correct.'

Mixed emotions gripped Kern. His aunt's words were uncomfortable and true. No one had forced him to leave and no one had kept him away. But even yesterday he'd chosen to leave a message on Eloise's answer machine, asking her to arrange for a vet to come, rather than go and face her in person.

'How could I have stayed when her second husband had a share? A share my mother gave him even when she knew it was a disaster to give anything to someone like him. Fin would have fought me at every turn.'

'So instead you've allowed him to destroy the place, panel by panel, nail by broken nail. Everything my parents and my sister gave to this place. The home and land your mother loved, same as your grandparents. All that history. You walked away from it because of a man not good enough to step onto this land, let alone be left with a free hand over it.'

Kern sighed as he took in his surroundings again. 'Better that than stay and be guilty of ripping it apart through fights and petty disagreements. Fin was never going to go along with anything I wanted or decided without arguing over it first. Better to start over than give myself a premature heart attack like the one that killed my mother. Besides, I didn't know it was this bad.'

'You didn't *care*, Kern,' Eloise said sadly.

Keeping a tight hold of the rope, she hitched the curve of her walking stick to the leather belt around her waist and lifted a tender hand to soothe the mare.

'Well, my darling. We know how that feels, don't we? When someone stops caring.'

'It wasn't that I didn't care—' Kern began, and the words were bitter on his tongue. He'd been raised to believe that he would inherit the whole property, but when his mother's will had been read he'd discovered that she hadn't only married Fin to keep his horses, but had also handed over forty-five per cent of the business. A business the man had no interest in building or growing. 'It was just—'

Eloise waved a hand at him, but when she spoke her tone was softer. 'Your dear mother hoped you'd be strong enough to grasp the challenge. Yet you packed up and left the day after the will was read. Sulked like the child you were. Married that cheap little opportunist—'

'Don't call my wife that,' he warned. He was aware that everything his aunt accused Corinne of being was sadly true, but he wouldn't hear a word against her. She'd had faults, yes, but she hadn't been completely to blame. 'She was—'

Eloise sneered, unhooking her stick from her belt. 'Just because the woman's dead, don't turn her into some saint. She saw ambition and talent in your eyes and she wanted to ride your colours. She was always going to be the ruin of you. All those years of work and she wrecked it all—just to spite you. You silly boy. You chose to be loyal to the wrong person, when this place was where you should have been.'

Kern opened his mouth to deny the accusation, but his aunt's words held too much truth. Nothing he said would make her understand his deceased wife's complex nature. Hell, he had struggled with it for most of their marriage.

'I still know people in the game, Kern. Don't try and dismiss what she did.'

Kern lowered his head. His aunt had never liked Corinne and she wasn't going to change her opinion. But she didn't know the whole story—no one did. Only he knew what had really caused his wife's actions that last day. Corinne might have caused the mayhem, but he was the one who'd helped to push her to it. That and the cruel reality that occasionally life denied a person what they truly craved.

'She's dead, Eloise.'

'I know—and I won't lie to you and pretend I cried tears over the news. But it doesn't change the truth that you ran away from your heritage and she made certain you stayed away. Until now.'

Kern swallowed hard, unable to deny it. He *had* run and, as Eloise had already pointed out, he was guilty of never picking up a phone or turning up for a visit.

'Well, I'm here now.'

'Yes, you are—though I do wonder how long for. Is this just a quick stop-off, or are you actually going to stay for a while?'

He didn't answer. If his aunt knew that he planned to leave as soon as possible, he hated to imagine her reaction. 'If you'll excuse me? I'm going to check on my horse.'

She nodded and remarked dryly, 'I'm sure some time outside will help clear that hangover you're carrying.'

He opened his mouth to deny it, but she shook her head. 'Don't be that liar I mentioned earlier.'

He moved towards the entrance, needing fresh air for more than just to clear his head. The stables, despite their condition, still held memories in every corner he looked. They stifled and taunted him. Reminding him of everything he had lost both recently and long ago.

'Did the vet come yet?' his aunt asked.

Glad for a subject other than raking up the past, he nodded. 'Yes, but Fin came out of the house and played up, so I sent her away.'

Eloise smiled mysteriously. 'She's arrived in Dorset, then? Good. Here—take this girl,' she ordered, holding out the rope. 'I rescued this sweetheart yesterday and I need someone to look after her.'

Kern sighed and reached for the rope. What did the woman expect him to do with the mare? The stables were hardly decent, clean or accommodating. 'Why can't you do it?'

Eloise patted the mare gently on the neck. 'I'm too old and all my barns are full.'

'With what?'

She shoved a hand into her cardigan pocket and turned towards the entrance. 'Things I doubt you'd be interested in. Look after her. She needs someone to care. She used to be a bit of a star once.'

So had he, Kern mused silently. One so bright he'd believed he would be star for ever. What a joke.

'This place is falling down and I have no bedding.'

Eloise raised her eyebrow once more. 'Then you'd best get busy rectifying those issues. You never used to be afraid of hard work. Please don't tell me that has changed.'

'Of course not,' he retorted.

He'd worked his backside off to achieve his dreams and no one could take that truth from him.

She chuckled and walked away. 'Good to see you home, Kern. I truly hope this time you find the gumption to stay.'

CHAPTER THREE

RUBY KNOCKED ON the frosted glass door of the 1960s bungalow, trying to decide if she might be better spending the remainder of the afternoon searching for a caravan site.

When she'd returned to the practice and explained the events at MacKinley farm, and Kern MacKinley's strange behaviour, her new boss had listened, then handed over half his afternoon appointments to her, stating she should consider them part of a practical interview.

Thrilled to finally be working, Ruby had enjoyed every moment of the consultations. And despite a nervous start she'd managed to treat the seven animals without any mishaps.

After her last appointment Anne had handed her a piece of paper with the name of a woman who would be willing to let Ruby park her caravan on her land for a small weekly fee. But then Anne had mentioned it was next door to the MacKinley farm and was owned by Kern MacKinley's aunt.

After this morning's carry-on with the nephew, Ruby dreaded meeting the woman. What if she was as bad as her nephew?

Ruby knocked again, leaning close to the glass to listen for any sign of movement from inside the building. Perhaps Eloise Blake had fallen asleep?

Anne had told her the woman rarely answered the phone, and it would be better to drive out and talk to her in person.

Finally a figure appeared through the glass and the door opened to reveal a dark-haired woman with silver streaks at her temples, leaning heavily on a walking stick.

'Hello. Are you Eloise?' Ruby asked, suddenly hit by an attack of nerves.

The woman lifted her chin and gave Ruby a thorough once-over. 'I am. You must be the new vet from town.'

Surprised, Ruby paused for a second. Had Anne contacted the woman and warned her of Ruby's visit? 'Yes. How did you know?'

'Psychic, dear. I read it in my daily horoscope. How a young beautiful stranger with a lip ring would soon come to see me.'

'Oh,' Ruby said, her good mood evaporating. Obviously the MacKinleys and the Blakes were all bonkers. First the unclothed nephew and now the mystic aunt.

'You think I'm batty, don't you?' Eloise asked with a smile. 'Most people do when faced with a subject they don't understand. Though I'd have thought you might think differently, considering your own special gift.'

Discomfort moved over Ruby for the second time that day. What did this strange old lady know about her gift? Had Alex Morsi spoken to her about what Professor Handel had apparently told him? Did others know too?

'I'm not—'

Eloise huffed and shook her head, giving Ruby the impression she had disappointed the old woman. 'I'm not crazy. It's better you understand that from the start or you and I may well fall out. Now, you want to set up home on my land, do you?'

Ruby wasn't sure any more—but time was getting on and she needed to find somewhere to park for the night. 'Is it possible?' she asked.

Eloise nodded and stepped out onto the doorstep. 'It is. I suggest you park your caravan along by the river. It's beautiful at this time of the year, and the weather forecast for the week says the sun is staying around.'

'I own a dog,' Ruby said, aware that not everyone liked or allowed animals on their land. She refused to stay anywhere Dog wasn't welcome.

Eloise slammed the front door. 'Not a problem. I like dogs. Better company than humans, in my opinion. Almost as good as horses. Let's take a drive down, shall we?'

She didn't wait for Ruby to reply. Instead, she walked past her and towards the car. With a quick hello to Dog, who'd stuck his head out of the open rear window, she climbed into the front passenger seat and slammed the door.

Deciding she'd better follow, before the old lady changed her mind, Ruby hurried over to the car.

Within minutes they were heading down a dirt track in the direction of the river.

'I ran the place as a campsite until my second husband died and left me with a right mess to sort out, thanks to his aversion to paperwork.

Still, he's dead and I survived.' She glanced towards Ruby. 'It's what we do, isn't it? Survive the trauma and move on with our lives.'

Ruby swallowed, but kept her eyes on the track. Something about Eloise Blake unsettled her. It was almost as though she knew things about Ruby's past—which was impossible.

'You'll be able to hook up to electricity,' Eloise continued. 'The old cables still work. Hubby number two had his faults, but he was good at practical stuff.' She pointed out through the windscreen to the land in front of them. 'All this belongs to me, on this side of the river. The other side belongs mostly to my nephew. I understand you met him this morning?'

Ruby nodded and turned through an open gate into a field. 'Yes, he wanted someone to check his horse over but then he changed his mind once I arrived.'

'He was being cautious, sending you away,' Eloise explained. 'Fin, my brother-in-law, is a difficult man when he's sober and worse when he is drunk. Don't worry, Kern would never allow a horse to suffer. He loves the creatures far too much to do anything so cruel. If he says its fine, then it's the truth. But I'm sure you wish you'd seen for yourself.'

'Yes.'

'Well, you'll get the chance soon.' Eloise smiled mysteriously.

A shiver waved up Ruby's spine, increasing her discomfort. Yes, the family was definitely odd.

'I will?'

Eloise smiled again before pointing to a spot not far from the river's edge. 'It's in the chart, my dear. It's all written there if you know how to read it.'

Kern threw a stack of crinkled yellowed papers, consisting mainly of old receipts, bills and circulars for long-finished special offers on equine equipment, into the large plastic bin he'd dragged into the stable office from outside.

Forcing every bit of his attention to the chore, he tried to ignore the complaints coming from Enticing Evie, his four-year-old filly, who was making it clear she wasn't happy about being inside the old building.

Giving the dusty room another weary glance, he felt his heart ache at the sight of all the neglect. This room had been the hub of the yard when he was a child. Often better kept and cleaner than the main house. The shelves had been filled with a variety of books on horse care, veterinary and training manuals. Each upright and in their proper place. Now the books were either missing or lying in discarded piles on the filthy floor.

His eyes rested on a pair of leather gloves abandoned at the corner of the desk. His mother's old riding gloves. He reached for them, feeling the leather dirty and stiff in his palms. These simple gloves had once been so much a part of his mother, he struggled to imagine her without them.

Was she riding around heaven wearing a pair? He liked the idea of her jumping over hurdles, encouraging her favourite horse to do better, while his father yelled out praise from the side.

His eyes stung as he stared down at the gloves. They'd been a Christmas gift from his father before he'd passed away. He'd been twenty-five years older than Kern's mother, but the age gap had never bothered them or caused any issues in their marriage. They'd loved each other so much they'd seen only each other's hearts and love.

How he envied them that easy, natural love. So very different from the one he'd shared with Corinne.

Was Eloise right? Had his mother truly believed he had enough grit and determination to deal with Fin—the man she'd married out of desperation when he'd threatened to remove his best horses from the yard and take them to her nearest competitor unless she did so?

Evie's objections increased, forcing Kern to move to the open doorway. The thoroughbred's head was up, and she was stamping the ground like an equine Irish dancer having a tantrum. She tugged against the rope attaching her to the metal ring fixed into the wall and her eyes rolled as her body trembled and flinched.

'Hey, pretty girl…' he soothed, moving closer until he stood by her side.

She didn't want to be inside the building and she intended to make sure he knew it. She was desperate to return outside to the paddock, where she considered it safer. But a storm was forecast for the middle of the night, and he refused to leave her out in the elements.

'I know you hate it in here. I do too, sweetheart. But you can't stay outside in the paddock. It's not safe, and you're too precious to me.'

He'd hoped having his aunt's mare in one of the recently cleaned stalls he'd spent the afternoon repairing would help calm his girl, but she'd refused even to acknowledge the other horse.

Kern glanced towards the open end of the stable. In the distance he could see the shape of a caravan. His aunt had texted him earlier to let him know the vet would be staying on her land.

Great. Just what he needed. Miss Ruby Day was a distraction he could do without. He'd lost count of the amount of times her image had drifted through his thoughts since she'd left the farm earlier. Those serious brown eyes, her sweet pink mouth and her shocked expression at his undressed state…

He smiled. It was a long time since he'd shocked a woman. Thank goodness she hadn't figured out that the real reason he'd struggled to get his jeans on was due to his trying to hide the evidence of his body's inopportune attraction to her.

He'd considered marching over to Eloise's to

demand she send the woman on her way—but he doubted his aunt would listen, and he had no right to dictate who stayed on her side of the river anyway.

He'd lost any rights by leaving and staying silent for nineteen years. Today, when he tried to justify his reasons for doing so, he couldn't. He *had* sulked like the schoolboy his aunt had accused him of being.

First anger and grief had kept him away from Dorset. But as the years had turned into five, and then ten, and more, it had been embarrassment, shame and guilt which had kept his feet in another part of the country.

The trouble was, not once in that time had he imagined Eloise getting old.

What had happened to her second husband, Ralph? Had he left her too?

Evie snorted in another display of irritation. Kern understood and didn't blame her. After the bloodshed she'd experienced, the last thing she deserved was more stress. The drive to Dorset in the horsebox had been just about all the confinement she could stand.

He patted her neck and made his way to the

opening. The coming rain scented the air with a damp fresh chill.

With a final glance back at his distressed horse, Kern stepped out into the night. For Evie he would face anyone and do whatever was needed. He owed her. And for her alone he would eat humble horse crap pie.

Ruby climbed onto the bed, balancing a large glass bowl filled with cheese and onion crisps in one hand. On the bedside table sat a can of ice-cold cola, recently purchased from the town's mini supermarket.

For the first time in years, she felt hope warm her heart. Today had almost been her definition of perfect. She had a job she wanted, where the staff treated her normally, and a beautiful place to stay. How long it would last, she didn't want to contemplate, but tonight she was happy, and she intended to enjoy the rare feeling.

When the time to leave came, she would pack and do what she always did. Move on without acknowledging any regrets. Start over again the same way she had since the day she'd left home at sixteen.

Only once had she stupidly risked trusting

someone with the truth of her past, and they'd repaid her by selling a story to the kind of shoddy newspaper only interested in a sordid headline and lies. She'd stopped trusting people after that.

The so-called friend had tried to make excuses, but Ruby had refused to listen. There was no excuse for breaking a promise. None. What was friendship or a relationship without trust? Since that day Ruby had kept to herself and kept her mouth shut.

Sometimes it had been hard, but thanks to a decent inheritance from her mother, she'd managed to finish school and move on to university. After a couple of years working at a cat rescue centre she'd decided to train to become a vet.

Today had made lots of hard work, eye-straining studying and numerous part-time retail jobs worth it.

Leaning back on the pillows, she gently eased Dog's nose out of the bowl before he swiped a mouthful of crisps. Loving the unusual lightness in her heart, she closed her eyes and smiled.

'Paws crossed, Dog,' she whispered, stroking his rough, furry head, 'that this time we get to stay for a few months…maybe even a year.'

Dog licked her hand as if to agree.

Whatever happened during her time in Dorset, Ruby had this wonderful dog to love. Together they made do. She happily confessed all her secrets, wishes and dreams to him, her best friend, knowing that he'd keep them from the world. He was her perfect confidant.

A heavy knock on the caravan door startled Ruby into spilling half the bowl of crisps over the bed.

Glancing at her watch, she saw it was after seven o'clock. Who was knocking at her door? She knew it wouldn't be her new boss or his wife, because the man had whisked his family out through the practice door as soon as the last client had left, muttering something about a romantic evening. Perhaps it was Eloise? But Ruby didn't see the old woman as the type to go galivanting around at night—even if it was still just about light outside—unless she was ill and needed help?

Ruby opened her mouth to ask who it was when the answer came via a familiar deep voice.

'Miss Day? It's Kern MacKinley.'

She growled and glared in the direction of

the door. What right did he have, bothering her after work hours?

Another knock hit the door. 'I know you're inside. I can see a light and I recognise your car from our earlier meeting.'

With an irritated sigh, she rose from the bed, leaving Dog to feast on the spilled crisps. Slamming the bowl down on to the bedside table, she left the bedroom and headed for the door.

Lifting a hand, she hesitated before opening it. 'What do you want, Mr MacKinley?'

'I want *you*, Miss Day.'

In what way exactly did he want her?

She rubbed a hand across her brow. 'What did you say? You're mumbling.'

Silence hung between them for a second, before Kern replied in a much louder voice, 'I need your help. If you'd be gracious enough to forget what happened this morning, I could use your professional advice.'

Ruby bit her bottom lip, not wanting to be gracious or anything else where this man was concerned. Just because she was staying close by, it didn't mean she was offering twenty-four-hour animal care.

'It's late. Can't it wait until tomorrow? Perhaps you'd prefer to speak to my boss—?'

'No, I need someone this evening.'

And then he said the words she couldn't ignore.

'My horse needs you.'

Concerned, she opened the caravan door and looked down at the man who'd messed up her morning and seemed set on ruining her evening. 'In that case, Mr MacKinley, I'll come with you. But you'd better not mess me around again. The first time I could understand, but a second time will get you blacklisted at the practice.'

Kern nodded and placed his hand to his heart. 'I won't. I swear.'

She was pretty in the early-evening light, with her make-up smudged and faded in places. The woman's beauty shone through because of her eyes. Large, shaped like a cat's, and full of emotions Kern knew better than to try to decipher.

If he did, he might risk never being able to get free from the secrets that lay inside this woman's heart. He feared she had the power to bewitch him, and he was determined never to let that happen again. Once burnt, for ever scarred.

'It's a lovely evening,' Kern murmured, staring at the sky as they headed towards the river.

Anything to take his mind from the unwanted attraction he suddenly felt towards the woman walking by his side. His wife had been dead for less than a year—barely time for him to get used to being single again, let alone notice a pretty woman he'd best avoid.

Ruby nodded and shifted her medical bag from her left hand to her right. He'd offered to carry it for her, but she'd refused and gripped it tighter.

'But there's a storm heading for us in a few hours,' he went on, needing the atmosphere between them to ease. The last thing he wanted was for Evie to pick up on it. The sensitive horse was skittish enough.

Ruby glanced up at the evening sky. 'How can you tell?'

'You can smell it in the air,' he said, taking a deep breath through his nose before letting it out of his mouth.

She sniffed the air like a suspicious child

might smell an unwrapped sweet. 'Really? All I can smell is grass.'

'It's going to be a heavy one,' he said.

'You get all that from sniffing the air?' she asked, intrigued.

He smiled her way. 'Experience. I'm a country boy, remember?'

She gave the sky another doubtful look, then asked, 'What's wrong with your horse, Mr MacKinley?'

'Call me Kern,' he invited.

'I prefer to call clients by their surnames,' she replied primly. 'You said earlier she wasn't sick. Yet now you're calling on me out of hours to see her.'

'No, she isn't sick. Not in a physical way. My girl's more heart sick.'

Ruby stopped and stared at him. 'What happened?'

Kern let out a heavy sigh. 'Evie has recently developed an aversion to staying inside a stable. I was hoping you might have something in that case of yours that might help calm her for a few hours. Just until the storm passes and tomorrow comes.'

'Shouldn't she be used to staying inside?' Ruby asked.

Kern nodded. 'She was, but a few months ago she had a fright, and since then she hates being anywhere near a stable.'

'How did she cope travelling in the horse-box?'

Kern rubbed his jaw ruefully at the question. 'We stopped—a lot. But it's not the horsebox that's the problem—just the stable. And despite the one here not being up to much, it has a roof and walls, and smells enough like a stable for Evie to hate it.'

'Sounds like she's suffering from stress.'

'She is. But none of the paddocks are secure enough to leave her there during the night, and anyway my girl deserves better than being left out in a storm.'

'Okay. I'll examine her and see what can be done to ease her trouble.'

'Thank you, Ruby.'

'No need for thanks. Payment to the practice for my visit will be enough. Just call Anne in the morning and she'll tell you what you owe.'

He nodded. 'Of course.'

They came to the edge of the river and stopped.

For a moment Kern stared down at the water, trying to think of the best way to phrase his next suggestion. Finally, he decided straightforward bluntness was probably best.

He turned to Ruby. 'Unless you want wet feet and legs, you'd best jump up on to my back.'

Startled, Ruby backed away. 'I beg your pardon?'

Kern chuckled. 'You may want to close your eyes too, because I intend to take off my jeans. I don't want them to get soaked either. It's what I did on the way over to you.'

She hesitated, lifting her bag in front of her like a protective barrier. 'But—'

Kern placed his hand on his jeans button and popped it. Next, he pulled down his zip. The metallic rasp of it echoed between them. Kicking his trainers off, he tied them together and handed them to her to hold.

Ruby gasped and took another step backwards. Eyes wide, she spluttered, 'Honestly, Mr MacKinley. Must you keep doing this? If you dare lower your jeans, I swear it won't be your horse in need of medical attention, but you. Isn't there a bridge or something we can use?'

He almost laughed at the look on the vet's

face. God, she was sweet. A man might even believe she was as innocent as she acted. But Ruby Day exuded a fragility that suggested she'd once been deeply hurt. In a way only someone who had meant something important to her could inflict.

'My aunt had it dismantled the day my mother married Fin. I doubt she's had it rebuilt during the last nineteen years. Come on—for you, I will get my jeans wet.'

He fixed his trousers, turned his back and bent down, waiting for her to make a decision. He just hoped it would be the one that would benefit Evie.

A sharp, infuriated sigh signalled her agreement. 'Just until we reach the other side. Then you put me down.'

He nodded. 'Of course.'

The feel of her small hand on his shoulder sent a shiver of awareness and relief through his body. He bit back a deep groan when she jumped up and secured her long legs around his waist. God forgive him for the wicked thoughts going through his head, but he was only a mere man, and it had been a long time since a woman had wrapped any part of her body around his own.

Grabbing one of her legs to shift her into a more comfortable hold, he held on to the arm she'd slipped around his neck. 'Hold on tight. The water's not too deep here, but you don't want to fall in. And try not to hit me with that bag.'

She chuckled low in his ear. 'Make sure you don't drop me, then, Mr MacKinley, otherwise I might do it accidentally.'

Kern swallowed hard and stepped down into the water. 'Oh, I won't do that, Ruby. I'm never careless on purpose. Just don't fidget around and we'll be fine.'

She snorted. 'Make sure you're not. Or I'll make certain you get wetter than you did this morning. You should know I fight dirty when required, and I don't appreciate people who play games and waste my time.'

Kern chuckled and stopped halfway across the river. Water soaked him to just above his knees. This part of the river was shallower than where he'd jumped this morning, but still enough to be uncomfortable and cold, even on a spring evening.

'Are you threatening me, Ruby Day?'

'Just making sure you're the only one who gets wet tonight.'

Kern shut out the dirty thoughts her innocent words aroused and continued through the water to the other side. 'Hold on. The bottom's a little uneven on this side of the river.'

'Is the water still as cold as it was this morning?' Ruby asked, tightening her legs around his waist.

Kern groaned, forcing his footsteps on. Did she even know the effect her actions was causing? 'Yes. It's freezing.'

She laughed impishly. 'Good.'

Yeah, she knew. He'd bet his last pound coin on it.

Ruby stopped just inside the stables, her focus immediately drawn to the horse standing in the centre aisle. Everything about the animal screamed sadness and pain. Not in an obvious physical way that anyone else would notice, but a deeper, emotional agony that few understood or saw.

But Ruby did. And she felt it too.

Moving farther inside she saw Enticing Evie

shift, suddenly aware of their presence. Or rather Ruby's unknown one. Her tense, fearful stance and wide eyes were clear indications that she didn't want Ruby anywhere near her. This horse wasn't going to be an easy patient and she would probably resent any help.

'I'm going closer,' Ruby said, glancing at Kern MacKinley. 'It's probably a good idea for you to go first, though. She knows you and it might help to settle her.'

Kern nodded and walked over to the horse. Stroking a hand down her face, he crooned, 'Hey, girl. How are you doing?'

Ruby walked nearer, until she stood at the horse's side. The nervous filly stepped away instinctively, half turning to Kern for protection.

'First I'll carry out a basic physical examination,' Ruby said, placing her bag down on the ground, out of the way.

She opened it and retrieved her stethoscope. As she placed it around her neck she quickly looked Evie over, checking her general demeanour and alertness. From what she could see the horse seemed fine, other than mistrusting of Ruby's unfamiliar presence.

Stepping closer, Ruby inspected the horse's

eyes, nose and mouth. Everything seemed normal and her gums were a healthy pink.

'How's her appetite? Any cough?'

'Appetite's fine and no cough,' Kern answered.

Placing the ends of the stethoscope into her ears, Ruby listened to the sound of Evie's heart. Next she moved on to the lungs and stomach. Thankfully, everything sounded fine.

Fetching a digital thermometer from her bag, Ruby tugged the ends of her stethoscope out of her ears and approached Evie's rear end. This was when she expected the horse to make her displeasure clear. Many horses disliked the intimate invasion necessary for taking their temperature.

Giving the thermometer a coat of lubricant, she glanced over her shoulder towards Kern. 'I'm going to take her temperature now. Can you hold her steady?'

Kern nodded. 'Of course.'

Standing to Evie's side, in case the horse decided to kick out, Ruby move her tail to one side, gently pushed the lubricated thermometer inside her rectum and held on to the end. After thirty seconds, she pulled it out again and checked it.

'Her temperature is fine. As is her general condition.'

'That's good to hear.'

Ruby cleaned the thermometer and put it away, then turned back to the horse. After spending a few minutes checking her over from nose to tail, she asked, 'Is there anything else that concerns you other than her dislike for the stable?'

'No, not really.'

'Can you move round to her other side?' Ruby asked, needing him out of sight for what she planned to do next. 'I think it will also help if you untie her and hold the rope instead.'

Waiting until Kern could no longer see her, she slowly raised her right hand. Gently touching the horse on the neck, she closed her eyes and whispered softly, *'I'm here to help you.'*

Evie immediately stepped away, tossing her head in answer to Ruby's words.

'What are you doing?' Kern asked, suspicion colouring his voice.

He reminded Ruby of an over-protective parent. Would he be the same over his child or his wife? What would it be like to have someone act that way over *her*? Would she like it or resent it?

'I'm just making friends,' Ruby said. 'Seems only right after she's let me examine her. To have a little female getting to know each other time.'

Kern chuckled. 'You make it sound like a date.'

She lightly placed her fingers on Evie's neck again. 'Perhaps it is, in a way. Would you go to a doctor and expect him to just give you medication without talking to you? Or examine you fully and then walk away without a word? I just want her to know that I'm not all bad, even if I did stick my thermometer somewhere personal.'

'I guess you're right...'

Ruby stroked her left hand over the horse's face. Slow, calm movements meant to ease and relax. 'Always, Mr MacKinley. You should remember that.'

Come on, Evie. Let me help you. Ruby closed her eyes once again and mentally repeated the words, wanting to reassure the stressed horse that she could trust her. Some horses gave their trust quickly, whereas others fought against help. It all depended on the horse and what it had been through.

Resting her fingers with the lightest of touches, Ruby continued to talk silently to her patient, shutting out the noise of another horse softly snuffling somewhere in the stables and the bird-song outside. She cleared her mind of everything but the animal beneath her fingertips.

This time she felt some of the tension leave Evie's body. She wasn't fully relaxed, but it was a start.

I just want to help you, I promise.

'Can I do anything?'

Kern's voice penetrated Ruby's concentration like the prick of a pin.

'Like formally introduce you, or something?'

With a sharp sigh, Ruby opened her eyes and stopped herself from suggesting he shut up. She'd had owners like this before. People who struggled to be quiet and not interfere with the process. Worried they were somehow causing their animal harm by having her help them. Of course, Kern didn't know that.

'Would you mind fetching some fresh water?'

'Of course. I'll get some from the farm's well.

It's clean and drinkable. It's a fair way from here, though, so I may be gone a while.'

Perfect.

Kern grabbed a bucket and disappeared outside.

Finally alone with the horse, Ruby returned her attention to her new friend.

'Now we can talk properly' she said, patting Evie gently. 'I can make you feel a little better about being in here, if you'll let me.'

A sound came from one of the stalls and a brown head appeared over the door. 'See— even your friend there thinks you should listen. It's good advice.'

This time Evie appeared to consider Ruby's offer, and within moments Ruby's hand started to warm, radiating heat into the horse's stiff, defensive body. Instantly, visions of red and hot pain overwhelmed Ruby's senses. Whatever had happened to this horse had been ugly and raw. No wonder she was edgy.

'Oh, sweet girl,' Ruby whispered, a tear rolling down her cheek as she felt the pain envelop her. She couldn't see pictures, or clear images, but she could feel the fear and the sadness in the horse's heart and spirit. The intense agony.

Evie had suffered real loss and heartbreak.

The sound of footsteps broke into her concentration again, and with one final offer of love from her heart Ruby stepped away, pleased to see her new friend with her head down, looking more relaxed than when she'd first entered the stables. With luck, it would be enough to last for a few hours, until the coming storm had moved on.

'Here's the water,' Kern said, walking towards them.

Ruby nodded. 'Good. I think your girl's ready for a drink. She should settle now.'

Kern placed the bucket down on the stable floor in front of Evie. 'She seems much more relaxed. What did you do?'

'A little bit of massage,' she hedged, not about to admit the truth.

Her kind of healing was seen by many as some kind of hocus-pocus witchery and not proper medicine. But she knew it was. What she did dealt with the damaged spirit inside an animal.

'Some horses respond to it when they're stressed, others not so much.'

Kern continued to regard his horse. 'She's definitely calmer. Massage...?'

Ruby stepped away and retrieved her bag. 'She may sleep for a while. You might want to try her in a stall.'

'I prepared one earlier, just in case,' he said. 'Give me a minute and I'll walk you back.'

Ruby shook her head and wandered over to the entrance. The sun was low on the horizon and casting a pretty pink hue over the sky. 'You don't have to. It's not far.'

Kern led a much calmer Evie into a stall. 'How are you going to get across the river without your local piggyback knight to carry you? We're kind of a rarity in Dorset, you know.'

She laughed. 'I think this time I'll walk across, thanks.'

Kern closed the stable door and followed her outside. 'No need. Where are you from, Ruby?'

'Here and there,' she answered, purposely vague. 'No particular place or town.'

When they came to the river, Kern scooped her up and stepped into the water before she could argue or decline.

'I said I'd walk over this time,' she complained, but instinctively wrapped an arm around his neck and held tight.

'I know,' he said, moving through the water to the other side. Again, he stopped at the centre of the river. 'Of course if you'd rather I dropped you, just say.'

She gripped his neck tighter. 'When you've gone to so much trouble, that would be ungrateful and stupid.'

Kern laughed and shifted her higher in his hold. 'So you're a lady with no set home?'

'None except for the one I take with me.'

Reaching the other bank, he placed her back on her feet and together they moved in the direction of her caravan. 'Well, you certainly have a mysterious aura about you.'

Ruby frowned at his words, not sure how to take them. They sounded complimentary, but she'd never had anyone say anything like that before, so she wasn't sure.

'I do?'

'I'm sorry that I doubted you earlier,' Kern said. 'You must have wondered what was going on after that scene between Fin and I. Truth is, I haven't been home in a long time, and I'm not staying for any longer than I need to.'

'Does your aunt know?' Ruby asked.

He shrugged and turned to her. 'Probably— deep down. For the first time in years I'm in a position to make decisions which affect only me and no one else. My being here is only to tie up loose ends before I move on.' He sighed heavily. 'Doesn't matter where I stand on this farm, I just feel the past mocking me.'

Curious, she asked, 'Why would it do that?'

'Because I have a bad habit of making the women in my life sad. And it's time it stopped.'

Not understanding, Ruby regarded this man whose spirit appeared dejected and tired. As though life had slammed him with trouble too much. It saddened her, because she knew that feeling.

'I don't know what you did to Evie. God knows, I'm going to spend the rest of the night trying to figure it out. But you did something while I was fetching the water. Of that I'm sure.'

Ruby shrugged and glanced away. She didn't like not telling the complete truth, but she refused to give him a reason to dismiss her gift as nonsense when he'd already seen its effect.

'I just talked to her and massaged her a little. It was hardly anything. In fact, forget about making any payment to the practice. Consider it a neighbour's freebie.'

'Thanks, but I know it was more than that,' he said, stepping closer. He touched Ruby's face and turned it to him. 'Your eyes are pools of secrets, aren't they? You're too enticing for a man like me.'

'I am?'

He winked and tilted his head. 'Goodnight, Ruby.'

A shiver ran over her skin as he disappeared back across the river. Kern MacKinley saw too much, and from now on she had to make certain that where she was concerned he saw no more.

CHAPTER FOUR

'OKAY, I'M HERE. What's wrong?' Kern panted, having run over from the stables to his aunt's place after receiving a text message demanding his immediate presence.

Eloise stopped hunting through a bundle of old leather tack and smiled. 'Nothing. I just need your help with clearing this place.'

Kern glanced around the barn, packed with boxes and long-abandoned pieces of furniture, all the tat a person tended to accumulate after years of living in the same place, and almost groaned. *This* was the reason she'd called him over? A barn full of rubbish that had probably sat here for decades?

'Why?'

'Because,' Eloise replied cryptically. 'And as you have time right now, seeing as you're still undecided about your future, I figured you'd be glad to help. Besides, it will save you from having to do it when I depart for the next world.'

Kern sank down on a nearby stool and wiped his sweaty forehead. 'You're not going anywhere, so why the rush?'

Eloise peered at him. 'Who knows what's in store for me—or you—but I want this done. Move this lawnmower, will you?'

He stood and lifted the mower, which looked like a relic from the Edwardian era, and dumped it out of his aunt's way. 'Why the sudden urge to spring clean?'

His aunt returned her attention to the tack. 'I need the room.'

He again glanced around the barn. 'For what?'

'You are a Nosy Nicholas today, aren't you?' Eloise tutted, tugging on a leather bridle before tossing it back into the box. 'I just want your help, Kern. Not your opinion.'

'Forget I asked.' Kern remembered from his childhood that when his aunt was in this mood it was better just to do what she wanted. 'Where should I start?'

'You can put this old tack by the door,' she said, shoving the box towards him. 'It's old, but with a good cleaning it will be as good as anything you can buy. It belongs to you, anyway.'

He lifted several pieces out of the box and inspected it. His aunt was right. Although it was old, it was in good nick.

He glanced at her with suspicion. 'It does?'

'Yes.' Eloise nodded and waved a hand towards it. 'I borrowed it from your mother, along with a few other bits and bobs, after she died.'

Kern stared at his aunt. '*After* she died?'

Eloise picked at the top button of her cardigan. 'The day after the reading of the will, actually. You'd run off, and Fin was in London, no doubt trying to find some way to break the terms of the will. So I went over to the house and the stables with a van and...borrowed a few things.'

Kern took in all the boxes cluttering the area for a third time. Slowly, he recognised several pieces of furniture that had used to belong to his mother. Family heirlooms from his grandparents' time. 'You *borrowed* them?'

'Just until you came home,' Eloise said, flashing him a bright smile. 'Well, I wasn't going to leave it all for Fin to sell off, was I? You can go through it and decide what you want to keep and take back to the farm with you. The rest you can chuck out. Of course I never imagined I would be storing it for so long.'

Kern decided it was time for him and Eloise to get a few things straight.

'It wasn't that I didn't care about the farm. I just had to get away. Without Mum it felt wrong to be here. And, even though I was young, I had sense enough to understand that trying to run a business with Fin would never have worked. There was also a part of me that wanted to prove I could make it on my own. I worked my way from stable boy to boss and I'm proud of that fact.'

'Your mother would have been proud too, you know,' Eloise said. 'Of everything you've achieved. Even though it wasn't here at the farm, she still would have been proud.'

A hard lump formed in Kern's throat at his aunt's well-meant words. It was praise he didn't want to hear—not when he had fallen so far.

'Well, she would have something to say about where I am now, I'm sure.'

'She would have said that at the bottom of no-where there's only one way to go. Back to the top of somewhere. Where you really belong.'

Kern sighed and focused on the box of tack. 'Who says I want to go back?'

'Horses and racing fuel your blood, Kern,' his

aunt insisted. 'No point in denying that truth. What are you going to do if not train horses?'

That was a question he had no answer for. 'I'm not sure. I haven't decided.'

'There's nothing to decide. Can you really see yourself in a nine-to-five job, stuck in an office somewhere? You're down, Kern, but you're not finished. Not you—never you. You have land, the farm and a good horse. One from good stock, from what I can see. I'd say you have it pretty fine for a man about to rebuild his life.'

Kern shrugged, not sure he wanted to hear his aunt's words of encouragement. Right now, the whole idea of returning to the racing world left bitterness in his mouth.

'Maybe.'

'No maybe. Training is what you were born to do. It's what your parents taught you. Stop wallowing in the past and get on with achieving the glory days of tomorrow.'

'Ah, here she is. Ruby, come in and see how little my nephew has accomplished in the hour he's been here. He needs organising and I bet you can do it.'

Kern glanced up from searching through the

umpteenth box of rescued belongings, to see the woman standing with her dog on the threshold of the barn. Dressed in black cut-off jean shorts and a black T-shirt with hearts, roses and skulls all over it, she should look like a Goth, but the red and white scarf tied in her curly black hair gave her a fifties rockabilly cuteness instead.

Eloise walked over to Ruby. 'I have some shopping to do, so I'll see you two later. If you're good, I'll bring you both back a treat.'

Kern waited until his aunt had disappeared before speaking. 'I think she still thinks of me as a child. Though I'd best prepare you—my aunt's idea of a treat is never the expected.'

'Not sweets, then?' Ruby asked, shoving her hands into the pockets of her shorts.

Kern did his best not to take in her slim legs and the pretty curve of her calf muscles. But he was male, and Ruby was an attractive woman. And it had been so long since he'd thought of a woman as anything but an unfixable dilemma...

He chuckled and shook his head. 'No. Far too conventional for Eloise. Years ago she brought me a children's book I was desperate to own.

She gave it to me to read, but when it was time for her to go home she took the book with her, stating that she had to take it back to the library the next day.'

Ruby stared at him. 'She didn't tell you it was a library book when she gave it to you?'

'Nope. Eloise was always kind of crazy like that. And when you're raised with the un-conventional, you miss it when it's no longer around. Though there's other people's type of crazy to deal with instead, I guess.'

Ruby moved towards him, her dog following at her heels.

'Has she always been interested in astrology?' she asked.

'Oh, yeah. My aunt is as bright as a wolf moon. Don't be fooled by the scatty act she likes to use when it suits her. She's clever, tough, and she has a heart so soft it makes whipped cream look hard. I'd hate you to think differently. How did she talk you into helping with clearing the barn?'

Ruby stroked her dog's head and smiled down at him. 'She offered to have Dog one night a week, so I can do a late shift at the practice.'

Kern lifted a plastic tub filled with horse

brushes and carried it over to the entrance, where several other containers and boxes were stacked. 'Are you always happy when you talk about your work?'

She nodded. 'What's the point in working at a job if you don't love doing it?'

Her words reminded him of his aunt's earlier ones, but he pushed the thought away. The future could wait until another day. Right now there was a barn to clear. Though where he was going to put everything he wanted to keep, he'd yet to figure out.

'What should I do?' Ruby asked, reaching out to pick up an old book. She blew the dust off the jacket and smiled. '"*The Long-Abandoned Farm*".'

'How apt,' Kern mused. 'Start anywhere you want. I have a feeling I'll be packing it all in the horsebox and carting it back to the farm with me, anyway.'

'You've been quiet for a long time. What have you found over there?'

Kern jumped down from the chair he was standing on, coughing as dirt rose up from the floor after his landing. Walking through the dust cloud, he wove between several crates to where Ruby sat on an old pine box at the back of the building, sifting through a dark wooden trunk.

'I'm looking at this,' she murmured, her concentration on the piece of paper in her hand.

Intrigued, Kern reached Ruby's side and crouched down. 'What is it?'

Ruby handed him a faded old newspaper cutting. 'This must have been important to someone. And look at these photos. Aren't they wonderful?'

Kern took the black-and-white cutting from her, immediately recognising the image. A larger one used to hang in the stable office— a proud token from his grandparents' time. In the photo, they stood on either side of a horse. The horse he knew had been his grandparents' first National Hunt winner.

'Do you know who they are?' Ruby asked.

Kern nodded and smiled. 'Let me introduce you to my grandparents—Tom and Ada MacKinley.'

Ruby took the piece of paper back and smiled brightly. 'Hello, Tom and Ada. I'm pleased to meet you. You look a little like your grand-father, you know?' she told Kern.

He glanced at the photo again, searching for similarities with the old man he remembered only as a booming voice and a loud laugh but seeing none. 'Yeah?'

Ruby traced a finger lightly over his grand-father's faded black-and-white image. 'Here in the jaw and the eyebrows. In the eyes too. You both have determination in your gaze.'

Kern didn't see it. Everyone had always com-mented that he took after his father in looks and his mother in temper. Perhaps now he was older it had changed.

'My grandmother would have said bloody-mindedness. They married when they were both eighteen years old. They bought this land with a dream in their hearts and a willingness to work for it.'

Ruby glanced up. 'Did the dream come true for them?'

'Yes, for their lifetime it did. Grandfather Tom bred and trained winners. My grand-mother ran the business side. The old man won nearly every cup and award you can imagine. They were talented and a team. It makes a difference working towards success when two people are willing to work for the same goal. They were good people.'

'They sound it.'

'They were each other's backbone and reassurance when times were tough or lean. My mother was the same with my father. But when he passed, I suppose she lost her anchor. She struggled to keep the place going. She only married Fin because he threatened to take away his seven racehorses unless she did. The farm was going through one of its lean times, with Dad and Grandfather dying within two years of each other and new trainers coming into the business—young and keen, full of enthusiasm and false promises. In the end there were too many obstacles for her to fight against. She lost a couple of big owners to men who were not only the preferred sex, but who also spouted the guarantees of wins they wanted to hear.'

'So she married your stepfather to save the business?'

'Yeah—a man she couldn't stand, but needed. I told her on their wedding day I would never forgive her—that I'd rather she lost everything than be married to someone who wasn't Dad.'

'You were close to your father?'

'I was his shadow from before I could walk. My relationship with my mother was never the same after he died. She might have saved the farm and the business, but she lost my respect.'

'That was harsh,' Ruby muttered.

He sighed and reached for a photograph from the trunk. One of his mother and father on their wedding day. 'It was. And, do you know, if I was standing in her boots today I'd marry someone to keep what I'd worked for. I know that now. I'll always regret not being able to tell her so.'

'She probably understood your anger.'

He nodded, then grinned. 'But I bet she wondered how the hell she'd managed to raise such an obnoxious, self-righteous brat.'

Ruby laughed and handed him another photograph. This one of a pretty grey horse. 'I'm sure she did that on a daily basis anyway.'

Kern touched the photo but didn't take it. 'Are you insinuating something, Ruby?'

Shaking her head, she struggled to stop the corner of her mouth from twitching. 'Never.'

Kern leaned closer, his shoulder bumping hers. 'Are you sure?'

Ruby met his gaze, a twinkle of mischief shimmering in her eyes. 'Well, I have noticed you do have a bossy way about you that I suspect you also had as a child.'

'I do?'

'Mmm.' She nodded. 'You're something of an acquired taste, Mr MacKinley.'

Not able to resist the challenge in her gaze, Kern murmured, 'Am I really?'

As though realising the danger her honesty had placed her in, Ruby returned her attention to the trunk. 'Perhaps we should see what else is in here?'

'Trouble, I suspect.'

Those brown eyes came back to him. 'Sorry?'

'Nothing,' he said, reaching for another newspaper cutting and purposely brushing the back of her hand with his fingers. This woman was far too tempting to ignore. 'Just talking to myself.'

CHAPTER FIVE

RUBY WAITED UNTIL Kern's full attention was focused again on the papers and photos before examining the strange buoyancy in her chest. She'd tried to ignore its presence while they talked, had determinedly fought it when his long fingers had accidentally touched the back of her hand, but now she had no choice but to acknowledge and investigate the strange, frothy fluttering in both her stomach and her chest.

It reminded her of the times when her mother had twirled her around in a circle and her stomach had rocked and swirled throughout. She'd hated and loved it at the same time. Half scared and half excited by the unfamiliar sensation. It was exactly the same feeling as the one caused by the man crouched next to her.

Was this what people called attraction? A stupid physical reaction that didn't deserve anything more than a quick acknowledgement before she forgot about it again?

Why did Kern affect her so strangely? Was it because she had seen him without many clothes on, or because he was one of the few people who treated her as a normal person? He didn't seem to see her make-up and clothes the same way others did.

It was a strange feeling to be regarded as ordinary. But since she'd come to Dorset it was slowly becoming her new normal. Kern and everyone at the practice acted as if she was just a regular person. They were not put off by the way she dressed.

But deep down she knew she couldn't risk trusting them, or falling for the niceness of their words and actions. Too soon the disappointment would follow, and with it would come the pain. There was always the dreaded pain. Better to protect herself from it—even if it did mean missing out on this wonderful lightness in her heart.

Attraction wasn't for her. In the past she'd purposely avoided such emotion, preferring to keep acquaintances—male and female—in the friend zone. At first because she'd feared her past would become known, but eventually because it was easier just to place everyone in the same group and leave them there. Anyway, between studying and working, what little spare time she'd had left had tended to go on sleeping and eating.

Besides, she wasn't even sure she liked Kern MacKinley very much. The way he sneered every time he opened a box or unearthed a piece of furniture was a clear indication that he saw this afternoon's work as nothing but a chore.

For a moment, though, when he'd studied that old newspaper cutting, she could have sworn she saw something like regret in his expression. She'd probably imagined it. Thought she'd seen something in him just because she wanted to believe that, despite his odd behaviour at times, he was a decent person.

'You okay, Ruby?' Kern asked.

Startled from her musings, Ruby glanced up to find him regarding her.

'You appear to be off in a private dream world.'

No, not dreaming—just reinstating some common sense. Attraction to anyone was a weakness which led to mistakes. She didn't want to repeat the hurt of misplacing her trust.

She'd survived it once—better not to test her resolve a second time.

He reached out and touched her chin. His long fingers were warm against her skin.

'Hey, where's your smile gone?'

She tilted her head thoughtfully. 'Smile?'

'That pretty one you showed me last night,' he said softly. His thumb slid along the curve of her jaw before he let it fall away.

She returned her gaze to the box and frowned down at the contents. 'I did not smile at you.'

'Yes, you did. Almost stopped my heart, it was so unexpected.'

'Shh,' she hushed, embarrassed by his words and the idea that she had done such a thing. She never smiled. She wasn't the smiling type. Never had been. 'Don't you know Goths never smile?'

'You did,' he argued, and leaned closer to whisper in her ear, his breath hot and ticklish against her skin. 'Maybe you're not a real Goth. Perhaps there's another woman inside you who wants to smile, but your strict Goth rules are suppressing her.'

She sniffed and wrinkled her nose. 'The same

way there's a normal man inside *you*, I suppose?'

'Oh, Ruby,' Kern said, placing a hand to his chest. 'Are you being sarcastic and mean just because I know you have a secret smile?'

'Just making an observation,' she insisted, reaching for a large black photo album.

She flicked over several pages, waiting for his reply. Her neck was still tingling even though he was no longer close.

'Oh, no. I know sarcasm when I hear it,' he argued. 'And your words were thick with it.'

She flicked over another page. 'Maybe you need to test your hearing, Mr MacKinley. Unless, of course, your problem is age-related—then there's really no hope. Though I did recently read that hearing aids have improved. Perhaps you should check them out.'

'Why, you…'

Before she could see the danger, Kern stood up, scooped her up off the pine box, threw her over his shoulder and headed to the entrance.

'What are you doing?' Ruby yelped as they headed outside into the sunshine.

'I think I'll take your advice and see if my

ears need cleaning. A good, thorough wash will
do the job perfectly.'

'Put me down!' Ruby cried. Whatever he was
planning, she guessed she wasn't going to like
it. 'Dog, help me!'

Her traitor of a pet leapt around beside them,
barking with excitement. Instead of saving her,
he just wanted to enter their game.

Kern laughed. 'I think he plans on joining
us in our dip.'

'Dip?'

The swine laughed again, wickedly. 'Brace
yourself, Ruby. Because it's going to be cold.'

Freezing water engulfed them both within
seconds, covering them completely as they
sank to the river's depths and then rose back
up again. Splashing and barking nearby let
Ruby know that Dog had joined them in their
dunking.

Spluttering, and filled with thoughts of revenge, Ruby splashed out for the man who'd
caused this impromptu wash. 'I'm going to get
you, MacKinley!'

Kern laughed and stumbled back out of reach.
His dark hair was plastered to his head and his
shirt clung to his body.

Flicking more water in her direction, he chanted, 'Look at you...all dirty. Let me help clean you off.'

'Keep away,' she growled, wiping water from her eyes. 'I can't believe you did that.'

Shrugging, Kern playfully splashed more water at her. 'I only wanted to cool down that hot, cruel tongue of yours.'

'Oh, I'm going to make you pay,' she threatened, moving towards him. 'You're going to suffer, second by second.'

'Come on, then,' he teased.

She charged towards him, but her soaked trainers sank into the river's muddy bottom and made hard work of it. Before she had a chance to reach Kern he dodged out of her way for a second time, causing her to spin and fall back into the water.

'Missed!' he taunted, laughing. 'Try again, Miss Wet Vet.'

She did. And failed once more. The man moved like a fish, not at all hindered by his wet clothes.

'Ah, come on, Ruby,' he mocked. 'You can do better than that.'

'I'm going to get you back,' she swore, already imagining the vengeful retaliation she would inflict upon him once they were back on dry land.

He chuckled and shook his head. Waddling over to her, he grabbed her hand and dragged her towards the bank. 'Come on, Ruby. Let's go to your place and dry off.'

She seethed, glaring at his back as he tugged her through the water and up onto the grass. 'I don't recall inviting you.'

'Surely you don't begrudge me a towel to dry off?'

'Actually,' she mused darkly, 'I think I do.'

He turned back to her and pouted. 'But I could get a chill...'

She bit her lip to stop herself from grinning at his fake pathetic expression. This man was just too adorable. That cute boyish face he worked weakened her resistance and anger.

He could have a towel—but he could use it outside on the grass. The last thing she wanted was Kern inside her home, dripping, teasing, and utterly far too charming.

'This is nice,' Kern said, looking around her caravan with obvious curiosity.

Every now and then he would pick something

up, study it for a moment, and then return it to
its place.

'Thank you,' Ruby said, self-conscious of
how small the space was with the two of them
and Dog inside the kitchen area.

Her attempt to keep Kern outside had failed
dismally when he had dived through the door
before she could prevent him, and now he stood
in the centre of the kitchen, surrounded by pale
pink cushions and mint-green-painted kitchen
cupboards, trying not to bang his head on the
dangling crystals of her mini chandelier.

Opening the cupboard where she kept her
clean linen, she reached for the top towel, smirk-
ing as she turned and handed it to him. 'Use this
before you drip water all over the floor. Why
you couldn't stay outside as I suggested—'

'Because then I wouldn't be in here and seeing another side to you,' he murmured. He
glanced down at the towel, then back up at her
before taking it.

She glared at him and tried to hustle him towards the door. He had a towel, so now there
was no reason for him to stay inside. Besides,
her own clothes were sticking to her, and probably revealing too much of her body.

'I get the feeling you want me to leave,' he said.

'You threw me in the river and pushed your way into my home. You're not exactly my favourite person right now.'

He nodded to the dog stretched out at his feet, looking up at him adoringly. 'Dog's happy I'm here—and besides, I'm still looking around your home.'

She folded her arms. 'It's just a caravan. Nothing much to see.'

'It's more than that, Ruby,' he dismissed. 'It's your home and there's everything to see.'

He wiped the towel over the side of his face, leaving a trail of tiny pink threads where he'd rubbed against his stubble, while reaching out for an old postcard stuck on a board near the kettle. It showed a picture of a famous race course. One she suspected he would recognise.

Kern pulled it off the board. 'Cheltenham. Nice course. Have you been there?'

'Yes, years ago.'

She moved away and picked up the fluffy lilac throw she liked to snuggle into while reading at night. Folding it in half, she turned away from him and the questions she sensed brewed in his too-clever mind.

She should have thrown the stupid postcard away years ago. She regretted not doing so now.

'I never took you for a racing girl. Show jumping, maybe, but not National Hunt.'

'You hardly know me,' she reminded him curtly.

She was uncomfortable with how close he was to the truth. What would the man say if she listed the number of other racetracks she had visited as a child, or the less public names of well-known people involved in the sport? Names only people deeply immersed in the scene would recognise.

'True.'

She glanced at the card, fighting the urge to snatch it from his fingers. 'I was taken there a few times as a child by my parents. It's just a silly souvenir. Nothing more.'

'They like horse racing, then?' he asked. 'Your parents, I mean.'

'They used to,' Ruby said with a shrug. 'They're both dead now.'

Kern placed his towel on a seat and sat down on top of it. Twisting the card in his fingers, his expression serious, he stared at it. 'Sorry to hear that.'

'It happened a long time ago,' she said.

Sensing he planned to grill her further, Ruby pointed towards her bedroom door, judging avoidance and escape to be the best idea. 'I'll just go and change. I won't be long.'

Kern glanced again at the postcard, his eyes narrowing. Nothing was written on the back, and yet it added another thread of mystery to Ruby Day.

He'd tried to ignore her, but every time they were together it was as though they had known each other for longer than a few days. Time with her felt comfortable and easy. He'd forgotten how relaxing being with another person— a woman—could be. His marriage hadn't felt that way for years.

Yes, Ruby was a riddle. Her reaction to the card told him there was more to it than just a few fun days watching the gee-gees with her parents. This postcard meant something to her—something important and not something she intended to share with him.

Why? What was it about this card or the place on it that she didn't want to talk about? Was it simply that the card caused her to remember happier times with her parents, who were no longer around?

Well, they all had secrets and past experiences they wanted to keep hidden, but for some strange reason he was curious about Ruby's.

Why had she been so secretive about her background the other day? She clammed up every time he asked something personal. Why hadn't she mentioned her parents had died when they'd been discussing his own, earlier in the barn? And how had she got that scar on her neck?

Their dunk in the river had removed some of her make-up and exposed jagged pink flesh. Was the story behind the wound what she wanted to keep quiet? Or was she just shy and wouldn't feel comfortable opening up to him?

MacKinley, stop letting your imagination play just because the woman doesn't want to share her life story with you. It's not as if you're sharing your own, is it?

God, no, he didn't want to scare the woman off with his tales of marital woe.

Hang on—what the heck was he thinking? He didn't want to do anything where Ruby Day or any other woman was concerned *full stop*. He'd learnt that lesson for life.

He'd returned to Dorset because he had nowhere else to go and he wanted to take some time to work out his next move. For the past few months he'd dealt with the fallout of everything Corinne had instigated and, despite what his aunt thought, he wasn't sure horse racing was how he wanted to spend the rest of his days.

Perhaps this was fate's prod to rethink and change course? Maybe there was something else for him? Though winning races hadn't been a complete waste of his time...

Kern looked at the postcard once more and frowned. He'd never won the Gold Cup, though. Cheltenham's coveted top trophy had never sat in his collection.

A collection he no longer owned.

He stood and tossed the card down on to the tabletop. With a final glance round at the warm and cosy caravan, he strolled to the door.

Getting mixed up with a woman, no matter how cute and tempting, was not for him. Women caused nothing but strife and heartache. It would be easy to want to get to know

Ruby better, to try and uncover her riddles and study her secrets, peel away the coverings around her heart, but he refused to hurt another woman again. Or, just as importantly, to allow one to hurt him in return. Better to leave now than risk battering their fragile hearts.

CHAPTER SIX

'YOU DO REALISE barbecued food has the potential to kill, or at the very least cause sickness and diarrhoea?' said Alex Morsi.

Ruby almost laughed at her boss as his wife threateningly swiped the air between them with a spatula. Over the last week the couple had often provided entertainment during work hours, but this afternoon they were all attending the practice's annual barbecue in the rear car park, and Kiki had been left in charge of cooking the meat.

'I haven't killed you *yet*.' Kiki smiled not so sweetly at her husband. 'Though if you add any further unhelpful scraps of culinary doom I'm likely to warm to the idea.'

Alex grinned down at his wife, losing his normal serious expression. 'I'm just informing Miss Day of the risks.'

'Don't,' Kiki snapped. 'I'm a very good cook.'

'You are,' Alex agreed, moving nearer to his

wife and slipping an arm around her waist. 'I just thought I would tell Miss Day—'

The spatula made another swipe, just missing Alex's nose. '*Don't*, Alex! You know what happens when you "just" something.'

With a final warning glare at her husband, Kiki turned to Ruby with a bright friendly smile. 'Can I interest you in a beef sausage?'

Ruby glanced down at the tasty-looking food on the hot grill, but Alex's remarks still rang in her ears. Edging backwards, in case Kiki decided to turn the cooking utensil on her, she shook her head. 'I think I'll grab a veggie roll from the buffet table. I'm not much of a meat-eater, to be honest.'

Kiki growled at the man at her side and began a torrent of threats that made Ruby wince. Backing farther away, she moved in the direction of the practice and safety, in case Kiki decided to act on any of them. Dog stayed where he was, in front of the barbecue, ever hopeful of snatching something or conning a sausage from the cook.

'Friends of yours?' asked a deep familiar voice from behind her.

Startled, Ruby turned to find Kern, dressed

in faded jeans and a dark blue T-shirt. A silly thrill of pleasure ran through her, but she quickly dismissed it. So what if the man was here? It didn't mean anything. Or at least, it shouldn't…

'Mr MacKinley!'

'Kern,' he corrected.

'I didn't realise you would be here,' she said, surprised to see him. Mostly the guests consisted of work colleagues and friends. Kern MacKinley was neither of those.

'Eloise insisted I come,' Kern admitted.

Ruby grinned and teased him. 'So you're here because your aunt told you to come?'

Kern shrugged. 'The woman has a way of making me agree to things when I have every intention of declining. It's a skill I'd hoped she'd lost while I was away.'

Ruby laughed, not believing anyone could make this man do anything he didn't want to. She guessed the real reason he'd come this afternoon was to make his aunt happy. Kern MacKinley might like to act all deep and uncaring, but sometimes he showed glimpses of being a sweet man.

Glancing around, she noticed another surprise guest, talking to Anne's husband, Harry. 'And your stepfather? Did Eloise invite him too?'

'It turns out Fin is friends with your colleague's husband and he invited him along.'

'So an unexpected family gathering for you?' she said, looking up at him to see how pleased he was at the fact. It had been clear during their exchange the other day, and from what Kern had said while clearing out his aunt's barn, that the two men had little time for each other.

'If I'd known Fin would be here then I'd have stayed away, no matter what Eloise wanted. Every run-in we've had since I came back has ended badly.'

'Probably best to just ignore him, then,' Ruby said.

Kern nodded. 'I intend to. Would you like another drink?'

Ruby held up her half-full glass of orange juice. 'No, thanks. I still have plenty.'

She waited for Kern to walk away and find someone else to talk to—someone more interesting—but he didn't. Searching for a different subject, she asked, 'How's Evie?'

Kern grinned, the warm light in his eyes softening his features, taking away some of the tension that seemed permanently to line his face.

'She's much better. I still haven't worked out what magic you used on her, but she's happier in herself and willingly stays in the stables at night. She and my aunt's horse are slowly making friends too.'

Ruby smiled and brushed back a curl that was tickling her cheek. She was pleased to hear that her short session with the troubled horse had helped. 'That's wonderful.'

'It is,' he agreed. 'And it's all because of you and the spell you cast over her.'

She laughed and shook her head, feeling warmth flowing into her chest at his praise, easing some of her awkwardness. 'No spell or trickery involved, I swear.'

He stared at her for several moments, not saying a word, but his eyes did the talking for him. He didn't believe her, and the flicker in their serious depths told her he wasn't done with finding out the truth.

Self-conscious, Ruby touched her neck, wondering if she was imagining things. 'Why are you staring at me?'

'I'm looking to see if your nose grows any

longer,' he replied. His eyes narrowed and he leaned forward, closing the space between them. 'No, I think it's as small and pretty as usual.'

Ruby's laughter caused several people to turn their way, but she didn't care. 'I'm not lying. I just spent some time soothing her and talking to her.'

It wasn't a lie. Her healing did soothe and calm. Just like humans, animals reacted to strokes and soft words. Evie was a horse in emotional pain, and normally she would have offered further sessions to help the filly through it, but Kern already suspected some kind of sorcery, so the last thing she wanted to do was arouse his curiosity further. Not when she wasn't sure how he would react to the idea of someone healing by using her hands and her mind.

A lot of people were sceptical about holistic medicines and practices, despite the fact that most of them had been around longer than modern medicine. Many of the old cures had simply been forgotten over time and generations.

'I wish I could work out what you're hiding,' he murmured softly.

Unnerved by his words, Ruby glanced away. If he knew all her dark secrets she doubted he'd spend any more time talking to her. He'd cut her off without another thought.

It was what had happened in the past, when people had either discovered her gift or learnt the truth about who her parents were and the lurid scandal of a world-famous, much-loved jockey, adored by the public for his humour and talent and his French model wife. They'd been the perfect couple in front of the camera and the racing crowd. Only behind closed doors the marriage had been one full of violence, affairs and cruelty.

She couldn't risk anyone finding out who she really was. They would either hate her for not telling them the truth, view her as being secretive and not to be trusted, or—worse—grill her over her parents' marriage in their quest for gossip.

She shivered and gripped her glass tighter. The old familiar urge to be alone with Dog somewhere secure was returning. But she couldn't leave yet. The party had barely started, and if she did it was bound to cause talk and even offence among her new colleagues.

Kern touched her arm with concern. 'Hey, what did I say?'

She blinked up at him, wishing she had stayed at home instead of trying to join in with the others. She wasn't a people person, preferring her solitary existence.

'Sorry?'

'You seem upset,' he murmured.

'No,' she lied, flashing him a smile she didn't feel. 'Just thinking about something. Nothing important. Why did you leave the other night?'

Raised voices interrupted them. They turned in the direction of the ruckus, which was on the other side of the car park. Eloise and Fin stood several paces apart, glaring at each other. Fin held a can of beer and Eloise a plate full of food.

'Looks like a family bust-up is about to kick off,' Kern sighed heavily. 'Some things never change. I'll be honest—*this* I haven't missed.'

Ruby didn't like the way her landlady appeared about ready to throw her food over the old man. 'Should you go over?'

Kern shook his head. 'I doubt my aunt needs any help. I've known grown men to shake when she gets riled up.'

'Even so,' Ruby said, concerned at the way the old couple were squabbling. 'It's ruining the barbecue.'

Kern grunted. 'Okay—but if she gets angry with me, I'm blaming you.'

Ruby giggled and shook her head. 'I'll deny everything. Go—before your aunt starts throwing mushroom vol au vents. I haven't had a chance to eat any yet.'

'Fine,' Kern huffed, capturing her elbow and manoeuvring Ruby along with him. 'But you're coming with me.'

'I think I should stay back,' she said, not keen to get dragged into his family's issues.

'No way,' Kern scoffed. 'This is your idea, so if anything gets thrown you can get hit first.'

Ruby gasped. 'Such a gentleman!'

'Oh, I'm no gentleman, Ruby,' he insisted flatly. 'I'd hate you to make the mistake of thinking I am.'

They reached the elderly couple just as their voices began to rise again.

'What's going on?' Kern asked, shielding Ruby slightly behind him despite his earlier comment, his stance both protective and thoughtful.

'Oh, here he is,' Fin sneered, turning his attention to Kern. 'The returning son and nephew. He left with nothing and he's returned with nothing—because he couldn't control a woman.'

'Keep your mouth shut!' Eloise yelled. 'You know nothing about him or his marriage.'

'Enough, both of you!' Kern scolded the bickering pair. 'This is not the time for tossing insults. Go home if you want to do that.'

'Why shouldn't these good people know the truth about you?' Fin continued, not listening. 'You always believed you were better than anyone else—your mother was to blame for that.'

'Don't you speak about my sister,' Eloise interrupted. 'She was an angel—too good for you.'

'She was a money-grabbing waste of time— just like *his* wife.'

Wife? Ruby glanced at the man beside her. Not once had Kern mentioned a wife. Where was she? Did she plan to follow him to Dorset? Why hadn't he ever mentioned her?

She took a step away from the squabbling threesome, the urge to leave returning.

'I said *enough*!' Kern yelled. 'No one here is

interested in our family's past and grievances. Now, behave or leave.'

Anne's husband, Harry, moved into the group, his expression annoyed. 'Fin, I think perhaps you should listen to the man and go.'

Fin slammed his beer can down on the buffet table, causing it to wobble. 'Me? Why not them?'

Harry shook his head. 'Everyone was having a good time until this. I won't have Alex and Kiki upset because I made the mistake of asking you to join us. You need to go home and have a good long sleep. You'll feel better if you do.'

'Damn people!' Fin swore. He picked up his drink and pulled a bunch of car keys out of his trouser pocket.

'You can't drive,' Kern said, moving to take the keys from the old man. 'You've been drinking and you're in no fit state to—'

'Give me them!' Fin snatched the keys back out of Kern's hold and hurried away before anyone could react.

'Let him go,' Eloise urged, grabbing Kern arm.

'And risk him killing someone?' Kern asked,

heading after his stepfather, who had amazing agility for someone in his seventies.

'Dog—wait!' Ruby yelled after the hound, who had left his pitch near the barbecue and was now intently following Kern out of the rear car park. 'Dog—heel!'

Racing after the trio, Ruby ran down the side of the building and reached the front car park in time to see Kern tugging on the driver's door of a rusty blue van.

'Fin, turn the engine off!'

The old man angrily revved the engine instead, while swearing and yelling at Kern through the half-open window.

Ruby rushed forward, intent on grabbing her dog by the collar before he ran any closer to the vehicle. 'Dog, *wait*!'

For the first time in his life, Dog ignored Ruby. His tail swished side to side as he bounded towards Kern, his focus on the man he considered his new friend.

'Dog! Stay!' Ruby yelled.

Still yanking on the driver's door, Kern turned at her shout and spotted Dog heading towards him. Letting go of the door, he moved in Dog's direction and yelled, 'Stay, Dog!'

The Irish Wolfhound ignored them both and continued to run towards Kern.

'Dog!' Ruby screamed, desperate for the canine to halt.

Fin suddenly shot the van into Reverse with a squeal of tyres and slammed into Dog, sending the hound flying into the air with a sickening high-pitched yelp, before he fell back to the ground in a rough-haired heap.

Fear stilled Ruby's blood and her movements. Dazed, she stared at her dog, stretched out in the middle of the car park, her brain struggling to take in what had just happened. Her heart beating loudly in her ears, drowning out all the other sounds around her, she stayed frozen on the spot.

Alex rushed past her and reached Dog first, crouching down to check him over with expert fingers.

'Dog…?' Ruby whispered, tears coating her lips as they ran down her face. As if in a trance, she moved towards her boss and shakily knelt down beside her best friend, dreading what she was going to find.

'Miss Day!'

Alex's urgent calling penetrated the fuzzy

buzzing in her head and she stared down at her dog, still not moving on the worn Tarmac. *Was he...? Please, no... Don't let him be...*

Swallowing hard, she glanced up. 'Yes?'

Alex held her gaze, pulling her slowly from the shock that was about to engulf her completely. 'This patient needs our help. He's alive, and that's all that matters right now. Okay?'

She nodded and roughly wiped away the tears. 'Yes.'

Kern crouched down beside her. 'Oh, God, Ruby. I'm sorry. I never meant—'

'Apologies and blame can wait,' Alex snapped. 'Our patient's needs come first. We need something for a muzzle, Miss Day.'

She nodded, reaching out shaky fingers to touch her pet. 'Dog...?'

The sound of ripping fabric barely registered—not until Kern handed her a long piece of blue fabric that looked faintly familiar. 'Here—use this.'

Without a word, she switched from owner mode to professional vet and prepared to muzzle Dog's mouth. Even the most affectionate and soft-natured animal could turn nasty when in pain. Prevention was better than a bite.

'His gums look okay...'

'He's alert, and seems to be breathing normally,' Alex said, proficiently working his fingers over Dog's rough-coated body. 'His pulse is strong, too.' Alex gently examined Dog's right hind leg. 'There's no obvious wound or breakage, and no sign of bleeding, but...' Dog whined as Alex carefully manipulated the limb. 'I suspect he's sustained a fracture. I can feel the bone through the skin.'

'Anne, we need—' Alex stopped as his head nurse handed him a blanket.

'Harry's fetching a trolley,' she said.

Alex smiled and took it from his friend and employee. 'What would I do without you?'

'Struggle terribly, of course. I'm indispensable.'

Alex placed the blanket over Dog's body to keep him warm. 'Ruby, you and Kern get down here and support this leg and his rear end while we lift him on to the trolley. No point splintering it for the few minutes it will take to get him inside.'

'Anne and I will take Dog's other end,' Kiki said, kneeling down next to her husband and placing her hands in the correct position to support Dog's head and neck.

Ruby took Alex's place and with Kern's help prepared to lift Dog off the Tarmac with the least disturbance and movement to her pet's injured back leg.

'Right, team,' said Alex, 'let's move our patient.'

Together Ruby, Alex, Kiki, Anne and Kern raised Dog's limp body on to the trolley Harry had fetched from inside the building.

'I'll wait out here,' Kern called as the rest of them moved indoors and through Reception towards the back rooms.

Ruby nodded, then returned her attention to Dog. She couldn't lose her four-legged best friend—she just couldn't. He was all the family she had. Without Dog she would have no one to love and care for, no one in her life who loved her back.

'Right, Miss Day, what do we have?'

Ruby studied the two X-rays lit up on the screen, showing different views of Dog's damaged leg, and pointed at the obvious break. 'The X-rays show a broken femur bone.'

Alex nodded and moved to stand behind her. After a few moments discussing and reviewing the X-rays, he asked, 'Have you done any femur repairs?'

She shook her head.'

Alex turned away as Kiki wheeled a sedated Dog into the room. 'Good. I've done plenty, so between us we'll soon have your boy sorted. This will be your call—I'll assist, talk you through it and monitor. Is that all right with you? I'm thinking a pin will work best. What do you think?'

Ruby twisted round and stared at her boss. 'You want *me* to operate?'

Kiki glanced between them, but didn't say anything.

Alex rolled the prepared instrument trolley over to the table in readiness. 'Don't you want to?'

'Yes, but he's *my* dog.'

Alex glanced across the room at her. 'Would you prefer I operated on Dog and you monitored?'

Ruby considered the question and realised that she didn't want anyone else to operate on her pet. If anyone was going to fix his leg, then it was going to be her. 'No, I don't think I would.'

'Good.' Alex nodded. 'I know I wouldn't want anyone else working on my animals, so I figured you'd feel the same.'

'That's because you're a control freak,' Kiki teased. 'Right, you two. Dog's all prepped, shaved and ready for your surgical prowess. Let's get busy, shall we?'

Alex stayed on the other side of the trolley, his gaze still on Ruby. 'When you're ready… Remember I'm here to answer any questions or help overcome any unexpected problems. But I'm sure you'll manage fine.'

'Thanks,' Ruby said, comforted by his words.

She walked over to the trolley, her heart aching at the sight of her anaesthetised dog laid out on the stainless-steel table, tubes coming from his mouth and body. Sucking in a deep breath, she forced all emotions from her mind and gathered her mental strength while Alex placed the surgical drapes over Dog's body. She was very conscious that the operation wasn't going to be finished in a short time.

Carefully feeling the swollen area of the leg, she said, 'I'm going to make my incision now.'

Alex murmured in agreement.

Ruby picked up the scalpel and made a straight cut through the skin and muscle. Using her fingers, she located each end of the broken bone. With gentle manipulation, she managed to realign both pieces of bone in readiness to put them back together.

'Looks nice and clean,' Alex said. 'Should fuse together easy enough once pinned.'

Ruby nodded, and carefully fixed a pin into place.

'Nice...' Alex murmured.

Ruby finished off by suturing the wound closed and covering with dressing, ready for post-op X-rays.

'Good work,' Alex praised her. 'I can see I made the right decision, employing you.'

Ruby grinned beneath her mask. 'Thanks.'

A sense of relief and warmth flooded her heart. Dog was going to be okay, and it seemed as though she had just passed some sort of test where her boss was concerned. Despite the circumstances, a small sense of pride filled her.

'Thanks, boss.'

Alex tugged down his mask and smiled. 'You're welcome, Ruby.'

* * *

'How is he?' Kern rose from one of the plastic chairs in Reception, his gaze taking in the exhausted woman dressed in theatre scrubs, standing beside her boss. An overwhelming urge to drag her into his arms and hug her tight gripped him.

'He's stable,' Ruby answered, her voice dry and thick. Suddenly her eyes filled with tears. She shook her head and wiped them away. 'I'm sorry. I guess it's just relief.'

Alex awkwardly patted Ruby's shoulder. 'Time for you to go home and get some rest.'

Ruby shook her head, not wanting to be separated from her best friend. 'I'd prefer to stay and monitor Dog.'

Alex ignored her and pushed her gently towards Kern. 'Take her home, stick her in a bath, and then put her to bed. After she's slept for five hours she can come back and check on her patient.'

Kern gave in to his earlier urge and hugged Ruby close. Liking the feel of her head against his chest, and not at all put off by the antiseptic scent clinging to her, he said, 'I will.'

Ruby sighed into his chest and muttered, 'You're very bossy.'

Alex chuckled. 'That's why I'm the boss. I can get away with bossing you around—at least until my wife corrupts you the same way she has all my other staff members.' Once again he looked at Kern. 'Take this woman home. If you return before the five hours are up, I will fire her.'

Ruby twisted back to glare at Alex. 'Hey, that's not fair.'

Alex smiled. 'Trust me to look after your dog. Now, leave.'

Kiki walked into reception carrying the baby in her carrier and a tray of food. 'I thought we'd eat some of this here instead of carting it home.'

'Has everyone gone?'

'Yes. It started to rain, so everyone grabbed some food and went home. I asked Anne to save you a cheeseburger. It's probably cold, though.'

Alex smile widened and he strolled over to his wife. 'This is why I married her. She's the perfect veterinary nurse.'

Kiki snorted and tilted her head. 'I thought it was for my kisses?'

'They're just a bonus.'

Kern watched the couple and once again felt the loneliness that had plagued him during the last few years rise and hit him harder than ever before. Why did some people find romance easy? When for others, like him, it carried a heavy burden of duty? And wasn't spending time with the woman in his arms now just encouraging fate to wound him all over again?

Stepping into the caravan without the usual boisterous welcome from Dog was too much for Ruby. For the first time in years a cold emptiness hung in the air, as welcoming as a stinging slap.

'Let me help you,' Kern offered, reaching to remove her jacket when she stood motionless in the centre of the kitchen. His fingers were tender as they slipped over the material and pushed it from her shoulders and down her arms. 'A nice shower and then—'

She touched his chest to stop him from continuing. 'I don't want a shower.'

'You'll feel better,' he soothed, tossing the jacket aside.

She shook her head, not wanting to feel better. Dog didn't feel better, did he? Her best friend was alone, and probably confused, and she wanted to be with him instead of being here. Not once since she'd picked him up from the rescue centre as an overlooked puppy had they spent a night apart.

'I just want to...' Her words died as the ache inside her grew bigger, making her whole chest hurt. Tears hovered, then rolled down her cheeks, falling and releasing the emotions she'd held inside since the accident occurred.

'Aw, Ruby, don't...' Kern groaned, pulling her to him. 'I'm so sorry. I truly am. If I could change what happened so that Fin hit *me*, I would. I promise you.'

Ruby instinctively settled deeper into the circle of his hold, reluctant to move away, needing this moment with this man. No one had held her for so many years, and although she knew she should reject this closeness she didn't want to. She wanted to grasp this moment of comfort, as selfish as that was, and hold on to it for as long as he allowed.

'I'm sorry,' she gulped, between aching sobs. 'I don't know why I'm being so silly.'

Kern stroked the back of her head and soothed

her. 'It's not silly. You love Dog and he's been hurt. Cry all you want.'

He manoeuvred them over to the sofa and pulled Ruby down onto his lap, enveloping her once more in his wonderful warm embrace, shutting out everything as she gave in to the feelings she'd kept on hold while she and Alex had treated her beloved Wolfhound.

After a while her gaze settled on the blue-and-white blanket Dog liked to have on the sofa. He'd had it since she'd got him as a pup. Tugging it over, she sniffed at it. 'This is his. It smells of him.'

Kern lifted a corner and smelt it. 'Yeah, that's pure dog. Cheesy paws and all.'

She snuggled the blanket closer and glared at him. 'You think it stinks?'

'It does,' he insisted. 'But I also know that when I lost the horses in my care I didn't get the chance to keep anything that belonged to them.'

'What happened?'

Kern didn't speak for a while, but finally he said, 'My wife was what some might call "highly strung". She suffered terrible mood swings and bouts of depression. Had done since her teenage years. These last few years she became desperate for a child, but it never happened. Physically everything was working fine with both of us, but she just never got pregnant.'

Ruby hugged the blanket closer as she felt the man's sadness fill the caravan. Not sure what to say, she murmured, 'I'm sorry...'

'When the first year goes by without a pregnancy, you start to question if it's going to happen... Two years in, you know something is wrong. But when you seek medical help and the doctors insist there is no physical reason for the lack of a baby, it's hard to take. Who do you talk to then? Where do you turn? IVF gets mentioned, alongside adoption. But Corinne didn't want to deal with either. She had a phobia of doctors, thanks to her father having dragged her to several as a teenager. Knowing her mental health history, they offered counselling, but it never helped. Often she'd miss appointments, or just rip up the referral letters and throw them away. You see, because there was no medical reason, she clung to the hope of one day having a child without intervention.'

'That's heartbreaking...'

'It is when you're the one watching the person

you love go through it. Living with her disappointment every month, feeling like a failure
for not being able to give her the one thing she
craved.'

'She had you,' Ruby pointed out.

Kern gave another dejected smile and continued, 'I'm afraid I wasn't enough to ease her
persistent yearning to hold her own baby. Anyway, I'd gone to Doncaster for a race meeting.
During the third race the police phoned my mobile. Apparently Corinne had taken the keys for
the tractor and driven it into one of the stable
blocks. She brought the roof down on the three
horses inside.'

'Oh, no!' Ruby gasped, the blurred sensations
she'd experienced while working with Enticing
Evie instantly came to her mind.

'Evie was in one of the paddocks nearby and
she watched the whole thing,' Kern said, un-
knowingly confirming Ruby's suspicions. 'She
must have heard the other horses' cries of fear.
Luckily, the other eight horses not racing that
day were in another paddock, away from the
house. Afterwards, Corinne set the destroyed
stables on fire and drove the tractor at Evie.
Fortunately, the fire had attracted the neigh-

bours, and one of the staff members I'd left behind, and they called the police.'

'Where's your wife now?' Ruby asked gently.

'She panicked when the police arrived and ended up flipping the tractor onto its side. She was trapped beneath it and died instantly.'

Ruby grasped his hand. 'Oh, Kern. I'm sorry. Why did she do it?'

He shrugged, and his arms tightened around her. 'I think the fragile pieces inside her finally broke. After all the years of depression and disappointment, she just couldn't take any more. Everything built and built in her head until it exploded. I'd tried to get her interested in the business over the years, but she had no real love either for horses or racing. I'd encouraged her to make friends in the village where we lived, but she'd fall out with people after a few months, or grow tired of their company. I'd told myself I didn't have time to cater to her every whim if we wanted to eat and keep our home and the business. Truth is, I ran out of ways to help her.'

'What about her family?' asked Ruby.

'Corinne hated her father, and her sister moved to New Zealand fifteen years ago—not long after their mother died. Her mother never took her role as a parent too seriously, and when Corinne's problems with depression started in her teens, she dropped out of her life for good. She had no one but me. I couldn't abandon her, too. God knows where she would have ended up if I had. We were together for such a long time. She wasn't easy, but you don't walk away from your partner just because your marriage is hard work. I'm not a man who quits.'

'It sounds as if your wife's problems were something neither you nor your marriage could mend,' Ruby said, hoping he wouldn't be offended by her comment. 'Not without professional help.'

Kern was silent for a long time, then he admitted, 'I tried in the beginning—but in the end I'm guilty of just giving up. Corinne had become paranoid about me cheating—I never did. I respected her and my wedding vows too much to destroy either with cheap, easy sex. But according to her, I never spent enough time with her. She resented my work and the horses. She was rude to the owners. Forgot to give me important messages. Our marriage became a mess of resentment and anger on both sides. But although it was hard, and the last few years were a kind of hell, dealing with her mood swings, I did love Corinne once. That love died somewhere through the years, but for a long time she was my best friend and my lover. She deserved my loyalty and I know I should have helped her more—but how do you help someone who doesn't want it and resents you even for suggesting it? How do you get someone to listen when they constantly tell you to shut up or walk away? If I'd given up the business how would we have lived? One of us had to work. It's easy for people standing on the outside to think there are simple answers, but there aren't. Not really.'

'I didn't mean to imply—' Ruby began.

'I know you didn't,' he said.

Ruby sighed and rested her head against his shoulder. His questions were similar to the ones she'd once asked herself. 'I don't know, Kern. How *do* you solve a puzzle when there is no clear, simple solution?'

Stroking a curl back from Ruby's face, he apologised again. 'I'm sorry. I never meant for Dog to get hurt.'

She clasped his cheek and shook her head.

'I know you didn't. It was a horrible accident. You were trying to do the right thing by stopping your stepfather from driving.'

'I don't have a great history of doing the right thing, though,' he muttered. 'Not where women are concerned.'

She squeezed his hand, wanting to offer even the smallest comfort. 'You don't have to hold me.'

He tugged her close, kissing the top of her head. 'I want to hold you. It's been a while since I've wanted to hold anyone. Just for tonight, let's forget about common sense and comfort one another. Tomorrow we'll go back to being each other's bothersome neighbour.'

'It's been a long time since someone held me,' she confessed, snuggling deeper into him.

'No recent boyfriends?' he asked.

'None.' She sighed, wanting to be honest. 'I find it hard to trust people.'

'It's tough, isn't it? Especially when important people have let you down. That's why I've sworn off relationships for life.'

'I doubt I'll ever get married,' she admitted. 'It's not something that's ever interested me that much.'

'It's not all hearts and chocolates, I'm afraid.'

Glad he understood, she squeezed his hand again, wrapping her fingers around his cold ones. For one night she would revel in the feel of Kern and his wonderfully warm hug. Tomorrow they would pretend it had never happened. Slip back into the undemanding roles of acquaintances once more.

'Close your eyes and go to sleep,' he urged, his breath warm against her scalp.

'Okay…'

Some time later, through the fog of sleep, she felt herself being laid down on the sofa. A few seconds later the throw enclosed her body.

'Sweet dreams, Ruby,' Kern whispered, stroking a finger along her cheek. 'I'll be back in a few hours.'

Ruby listened to the sound of Kern driving off, wishing with all her heart that he had stayed. But she had no right to want such a thing. The man's soul was bruised and torn, and he deserved peace and time to heal.

Sadness and guilt had coated every word he'd uttered about his wife—a woman obviously mentally unwell, but too stubborn, perhaps too afraid, to take the help offered.

How tragic for both of them. A horrible situation with no easy remedy. He had been right when he'd described it as something nobody truly understood unless they'd been unfortunate enough to experience the same heart-wrenching pain.

Tonight they had shared some pieces of their pasts, but it made no difference. He was just a client who'd offered her solace and support when she'd desperately required it. A battered man who would one day leave and start a new phase in his life somewhere else.

She needed to make sure she remembered that the only place Kern MacKinley could ever be for her was at arm's length.

CHAPTER SEVEN

'THE PARADE?'

Kern stared at his aunt, certain the woman had gone potty. Why else would she be ranting on about the parade the local town held once a year? A parade she apparently wanted him to take part in.

He trained racehorses. Or he used to. He also had several more boxes to clear out of his aunt's large shed before it got too late, and discussing a parade he certainly wasn't going to take part in was nothing but a waste of his time.

'Oh, stop fussing,' Eloise complained. 'It's half a day—and it will do you good to have something nice to look forward to.'

Kern rested his hands gently on his aunt's shoulders, shocked by the feel of their boniness beneath his palms. Another sign of the passing of time... 'Eloise, I'm not a four-year-old who requires entertaining. I'm a grown man, and I can occupy my time fine.'

'You'll always be a little boy to me,' Eloise insisted. 'Besides, you're not doing it alone. I've arranged for an assistant—not only to help you clean the old cart, but also to keep you company during the parade.'

Wondering which poor sucker his aunt had conned into helping, he asked, 'Who?'

'Your neighbour.'

His heart dropped. 'Fin?'

'I said your neighbour—not your squatter,' she dismissed. 'I've asked sweet little Ruby to help you out.'

Kern swallowed, not sure what to say. He'd avoided Ruby for over a week, since he'd dropped her back at the clinic after her rest. Not because he didn't want to see her, but because whatever he felt for her was best left undiscovered and ignored. He wasn't in a position to offer anything more than friendship to the woman. And a small part of him feared friendship with Ruby would never be enough.

Holding her in his arms, feeling her body against his own, surrounded by her warm womanly scent, did nothing but hike up his unwelcome attraction towards her. An attraction he daren't explore.

'And she agreed?' he asked.

'Of course. Unlike you, she is helpful, and she doesn't complain all the time. You really have become quite grumpy as you've aged.'

Kern ignored his aunt's comment and demanded, 'What did you bribe her with?'

Ruby might be kind, but she also worked full time and shied away from unfamiliar company. He'd noticed her discomfort after watching her at the barbecue before her dog's accident.

Eloise shrugged and admitted, 'I offered to doggy-sit on Saturday afternoon.'

Intrigued, Kern asked, 'Why?'

'I thought she might like to do a bit of shopping or sightseeing. Since the accident she's worked and then returned home each day with nothing else in between. I asked Anne, and apparently she spends her dinner hours going over notes or checking the animals. It's not right for a young woman of her age to have zero social life. I'm just being neighbourly.'

'Hmm...' Kern murmured, not believing his relative.

Eloise clearly had plans stewing in her head, and he suspected the innocent vet would be too polite to refuse his aunt and would end up regretting the inevitable outcome.

'And she said yes, did she?' he asked, irritated by his own curiosity.

What the woman did and with whom was nothing to do with him. If she wanted to date all the men for a mile around, then good luck to her. Ruby was young, pretty and sweet. Any man with more than a handful of brain cells would snatch her up.

Any man who didn't screw up every important relationship in his life…

'Of course. Though I've yet to mention the parade to her. I thought I'd wait and see how you fancied it first. It will be a good chance for Ruby to get to know more people in the town.

'The answer's still no.'

Eloise huffed. 'You've developed a hardness since you left,' she complained. 'It's quite annoying.'

'Yeah, well, life will do that,' Kern replied, retrieving an empty bucket.

It was the reason he had to keep a distance between him and a certain vet. Ruby merited someone who viewed the future as exciting and worth exploring. He saw it as just something to be lived through.

'Is there anything else, or can I get back to work?'

Eloise glanced around the practically empty shed. 'You're doing a good job. Both here and the barn are far tidier. The stables on the farm are looking better too. When do you plan to make a start on the gallops?'

'When I earn some extra money,' he said. 'They're on the list of things to be sorted.'

'I can lend you some—'

'No, thanks,' he cut in, before she made a full offer. He still had a few fragments of pride. Besides, how could he take her money when he planned to move on once he'd got the place tidied up?

'Stubborn—just like your mother,' Eloise complained. 'But it's probably a good thing. Made you strong in mind and nature.'

'I'm still not driving the cart in any parade,' he insisted, not trusting his aunt's compliments or offers of help when she was set on getting her own way. This time he was determined to deny her, no matter what she said or did.

'Think about it, won't you?' Eloise begged.

'You know how to drive it from when your father taught you as a teenager. I'm sure it will all come back to you.'

The memory made him smile—until he noticed his aunt's pleased expression and felt a new wave of resolve grip him. 'No.'

'It'll mean you get to spend some time with a certain Miss Ruby Day.'

His heart kicked at the thought, but he busied himself reaching for several boxes of screws. He was glad for another reason to refuse. Less time with Ruby was better for his head—and a couple of other parts of his anatomy. Parts best left in their customary dormant condition.

'I doubt she wants to see me,' he said.

'I think you're wrong,' Eloise argued, following him to the shed's entrance.

Kern really didn't want to hear any more. He'd already spent far too much time thinking about Ruby, and he refused to do anything further...like develop strong feelings for her. The last thing she'd desire was a man like him in her life.

He sighed and reminded his aunt, 'Her dog has a broken leg because of me. If I hadn't rushed after Fin, poor Dog would be running around just fine.'

Eloise shook her head. 'It was an accident. It's my fault as much as yours, and Fin's really the one to blame. If she's going to be upset with anyone, it should be him.'

'It's also less than a year since I lost my wife, and I feel no desire to form any kind of a new relationship.'

So why do those words feel like a lie, MacKinley? Why do you wake up every damn morning aching to hold Ruby? Why do you feel restless each evening when you glance across the river and watch the light in her caravan window? Wondering what she's doing and how she's feeling. Wishing you could spend the evening with her.

'I'm still getting used to the single life. It might be fun to enjoy it for a year or two.'

Liar. That's how you felt before Ruby. Now you don't know how you feel.

Kern dropped the screws into the bucket with a thud. Where Ruby was concerned, he didn't know what he wanted. Though his excuses wouldn't hold much water with his aunt if she ever knew that he and Corinne had stopped sharing anything meaningful years ago.

He'd offered her a divorce many times over the years, but she'd always refused. Gradually, their relationship and love had faded into monthly sex and a diminishing friendship.

She'd blamed *him* for their lack of children, even though the doctors had insisted they were both capable of producing them. As the years had passed Corinne had convinced herself it was his fault, even though there had been no logic or evidence to support her accusation.

Shaking off the past, Kern glanced at his aunt. 'Ruby deserves to spend time with a man who wants a proper relationship. Someone whose heart is still intact and full of love. That's something mine will never be again.'

Sadness filled Eloise's gaze and she nodded. 'I suppose you're right. She is a delightful young woman. She'll probably meet someone at work or in town. I'm surprised the Baxter twins haven't asked her out. They're both searching for a wife…'

'Maybe you should tell her?' he suggested, forcing each word from his mouth. Despite not knowing the men, he immediately hated them—which was neither fair, nor made any sense.

'I will,' Eloise agreed. 'I'm going to put the kettle on. Come on inside when you've finished here.'

Kern waited for his aunt to leave before he let the bucket drop to the floor. He meant it. Ruby deserved the one thing he was incapable of giving: love. And he'd sworn the day Corinne died that he'd never risk becoming entwined with that emotion again.

Ruby hesitated outside the barn, listening to the bickering voice in her head, one of which insisted that this was a stupid idea. She should never have agreed to help Eloise. But the woman had asked in a way that had made it impossible to say no without causing offence.

As for Kern—she'd not seen him in over a week. The poor man was probably keeping out of her way, for fear she might throw herself into his arms and blubber all over him again.

What a fool she'd been, carrying on in such a way and exploiting his kindness. Too much of a gentleman to push her away, or leave, he'd suffered through her crying session with stoic patience. How cringingly embarrassing for both of them.

The poor man had lost his wife and everything important to him—and despite his admitting that his marriage had been seriously troubled, the last thing he needed was someone using his shoulder as a tissue to sob out her all her relief, worries and woes upon.

With a deep breath, Ruby stopped listening to the squabbling in her head and stepped inside the metal shed. Blinking as her eyes adjusted to the dim interior, she saw Kern standing at the far end next to a large, bulky item covered with green canvas.

'Hi,' she called out, heading towards him.

She refused to show any discomfort or any sign that the sudden fast beating of her heart was making her slightly light-headed. Maybe it was the way his grubby T-shirt hugged his body and showed off his powerful arm muscles. Why did he have to be so handsome, tall and hunky? Good-looking and nice?

A nice man who allowed a woman to dribble tears and a runny nose all over him. A fatal combination for any woman—including her.

Kern slowly turned to her, his smile unnatural and stiff. Ruby's heart nosedived in a sickening spiral to splat somewhere around her heels.

Obviously the snot and the ugly tears really were complete turn-offs and all too much for him.

Ruby swallowed and willed her stupid head to stop overthinking.

The man has no interest in you, Ruby, so get over yourself. So what if you've lost another friend? It doesn't matter. You're used to being alone—deal with it. It's life. Stop whinging and face it like a woman.

Ruby forced a smile in return, then fixed all her attention on the large object behind him. 'Is that the reason your aunt asked me here?'

He nodded and reached behind him for the corner of the stiff fabric. 'This is her latest project. Or should I say ours? Once I pull this cover off you'll see why I'm not dancing with excitement and joy.'

Ruby lurched forward and placed her hand over his to stop him from peeling back more than a small triangle of the canvas. Warmth rushed over her skin at the contact, and her heart attempted to elevate itself back up to her chest and regain its earlier manic speed.

She blushed at the unfamiliar sensation and at her own unexpected behaviour. When had she become so forward?

'Won't you let me try and guess what it is first?' she asked, her voice husky and rushed.

Kern stared at her for a second, before slowly grinning. 'Fine—but you'll never get it.'

'Bet I will,' she disputed, relieved that his awkwardness had disappeared and the uncomfortable air between them had gone with it. He might not find her attractive, but they could still be friendly.

'Okay. You get two guesses.'

She frowned and rested her hands on her hips. 'Two? Why not three?'

'Because I like the odds in my favour,' he said smugly. 'Shut your eyes and let's start.'

'Must I close my eyes?' she hedged, suddenly unsure.

The man had dumped her in the river before. Could she trust him not to do something just as unscrupulous when her eyes were shut?

Though the idea of being in his arms again wasn't unappealing...

His smile turned wicked and teasing. 'Many things are far more fun if you close your eyes, Ruby.'

She raised an eyebrow. 'Sounds dangerous.'

His lips twitched higher and his playful gaze morphed into a dark smoulder. 'We all need a little danger sometimes.'

With a murmur, Ruby closed her eyes and tried to calm her pounding heart. Suddenly she was happy to experience a little danger, if Kern insisted on it. Her life was so safe and empty of fun...sometimes she hurt from the loneliness of it.

Watching couples from afar, seeing them laugh and play emphasised how little close physical contact she shared with anyone. There was no one for her to discuss the news with, or talk to about what had occurred in the latest TV drama. It made for a staid existence at times. If it wasn't for Dog she'd experience no real happiness and companionship at all.

'Raise your hand,' Kern murmured close to her ear.

His breath tickled and she bit her lip to stop herself from laughing and squirming on the spot.

She lifted her hand and he gently guided her fingers over the canvas and rested them on top. She wrinkled her nose. 'Can I ask questions before I guess?'

He shifted until his chest pressed into her back, his body's heat warming her shoulder blades. 'If you want to—but only two.'

Stroking her fingertips lightly over the rough fabric, she frowned. 'Does the canvas have anything to do with what's underneath?'

'No.'

She frowned harder, searching for a hint from the hard lump beneath her palm. Conscious of not wanting to waste her last question, she asked, 'Is there a connection with horses?'

He chuckled, his fingers twitching slightly over her own. 'Yes, there is. Without a horse this item would be useless.'

Intrigued, she searched her mind for ideas of what it might be. She'd asked about a connection with horses only because of Kern's and Eloise's close ties with the equine world. Other than that, she didn't have any idea.

'Well?' he asked.

'No idea,' she admitted, irritated that she couldn't decipher anything from the bulges, thanks partly to his distracting presence. How was she supposed to concentrate when he enclosed her so completely?

'Do I get a clue?' she asked hopefully.

He laughed dryly. 'No. You've already asked your two questions. Time to guess.'

'You're mean,' she complained.

Kern agreed. 'Open your eyes and let me show you what it is.'

She did, and her eyes immediately took in the sight of their hands still connected on the green fabric—his dark and life-worn, hers paler and softer, thanks to the hand cream she used every night before bed. What would he do if she lifted her fingers slightly and linked them with his? Would he pull away or slip his own into hers?

'Last chance,' he pronounced against the curve of her ear.

With a final glance over the mysterious item's length, she uttered the first thing that came into her head. 'A sleigh?'

'Close.' Kern tugged off the canvas covering to reveal a very old and sad-looking Victorian cart.

'Wow…' she whispered, taking in the two large wheels. Her imagination immediately pictured a young woman on the wooden seat, driving around town, making deliveries or visiting friends. 'It's lovely,' she declared softly.

Kern grunted. 'It's tired and in need of a good clean. Which is what my aunt wishes us to give it. She's nagging at me to drive it in the town parade. This year's theme is Victoria and Albert, apparently.'

'Really?' Ruby asked, visualising Kern dressed like a Victorian farmer, cantering along the country roads, waving and calling out to passing neighbours or grazing livestock.

'My father used to compete in cart driving competitions, and he taught me how to drive this thing years ago. I'm surprised my aunt hasn't sold it.'

Ruby slowly walked around the cart, taking in the large spindly wheels and peeling paint. A piece of wood across the back section had split and required repair, but it was still lovely in a shabby, aged way.

She slipped a hand over one of the long wooden shafts. 'Is it safe to use?'

Kern regarded the antique vehicle. 'It used to be—despite its fragile appearance. I'll give it a good check-over after we brush off the cobwebs and wash it down.'

'Can we pull it outside?' Ruby asked, wanting to get a better look at this relic from the past.

She understood Eloise's wish for her nephew to take part in the parade. She would happily stand on a crowded pavement for a brief glimpse of Kern driving past, looking all dapper and gorgeous.

Kern sighed and handed her the bucket, now minus the screws. 'You fetch the water and I'll move it outside.'

Ruby clapped her hands before rushing towards the door, all her earlier worry forgotten thanks to the cart. 'A new coat of paint won't take long to apply, you know...'

Kern dragged the canvas farther back, until it folded onto the floor in a heap. 'It probably needs woodworm treatment first.'

'Sounds good,' Eloise declared as she joined them. 'There's some black paint in the other shed. You know what else would be good, Ruby?'

Ruby shook her head, her gaze still on the cart. 'No? What?'

'Oh, God...' Kern groaned, convinced he knew where his aunt was heading.

Eloise shot him a glare. 'If you and Kern dressed as a Victorian courting couple and did the parade together. Oh, how wonderful you'd look, sat together on the seat, clip-clopping along... We could twine real flowers on the sides and dress Star in brasses and ribbons. You'd look spectacular.'

'No,' Kern refused, scowling at his aunt.

Until a soft, disappointed 'Oh...' from the other side of the shed reached his ears.

Reluctantly, he turned, and saw that Ruby's expression matched her dejected tone.

'Don't be a nuisance, nephew,' Eloise scolded, sending Kern a triumphant glance. 'Can't you see how excited Ruby is to do it? Are you really so selfish as to deny her?'

Kern glanced Ruby's way again and asked, 'Do you really want to do the parade? Dressing up and everything?'

Ruby grinned and nodded shyly. 'It sounds

fun. I've never taken part in a parade... But if you'd rather not, I understand.'

Still feeling cantankerous, but hating Ruby's crushed expression, he sighed. 'All right. I'll help you paint it and I will *consider* taking part in the parade—'

'Wonderful!' Eloise cried. 'Why don't you both discuss it further over dinner?'

'B-but—' Ruby stammered, glancing Kern's way.

The man's face had suddenly taken on an expression similar to that of a person suffering painful cramp.

'Ruby probably has plans,' Kern said, flashing a glare at his aunt.

Eloise ignored him and asked, '*Do* you have plans, Ruby?'

'Well, no...' she answered, not willing to lie, though it was clear Kern wasn't keen on the idea of spending the evening with her.

'Then Kern would love to take you out for dinner tonight. Wouldn't you, nephew?'

Kern shot another black look at his aunt and cleared his throat. 'Ruby, would you like to go to dinner with me? I can't promise to be great company because it's been a while since I shared an evening out, but I'll try my best.'

'I—I—' Ruby was stammering again, shocked that he was letting his aunt manoeuvre him into asking. But then the woman did have a forceful directness that left a person struggling against her wishes. Feeling sorry for him, Ruby said, 'That's very kind of you, Kern. But you don't have to—'

'I want to,' he said, though his expression indicated the complete opposite.

'Can you afford it?' she asked, wanting to give him a way out.

This time he glared at her. 'Of course I can!'

She glanced in Eloise's direction. 'I don't want you to feel you have to because—'

'I don't,' he interrupted, getting her meaning. 'In fact, the more I think it over, the more I want to take you out. We're friends, aren't we? It will make a nice change from eating a pot of tasteless noodles. Unless you'd rather not spend time in my company? If you'd prefer to refuse, then just say so.'

Feeling reckless and a little mischievous, Ruby grinned. After all, she still owed him payback for that dunking in the river the other day. Why not get revenge and a full stomach at the same time?

'I'd love to,' she said. 'But nowhere fancy. I'm not into anywhere with more cutlery on the table than food on the plate.'

He grunted. 'Good. Because I know the perfect place.'

She was going out to dinner with a man. No, not any man, but Kern MacKinley. Oh, God, what would they talk about? The weather? Animals? What if she dropped food down the front of her top and spent the whole evening with a large ugly mark on her chest? Though, wearing black, it wouldn't really show.

Not that she cared about impressing the man, but displaying a lack of basic table skills was bound to prevent him from ever asking again. Not that he'd planned to this time. Without his aunt's prodding and interference they would both be spending the evening alone and stain-free.

Going out with a man who, through his work, must have often shared the company of the rich and famous sounded stressful. How lacking would he find her conversation? How soon before he started to rush her through the meal, desperate for an end to the pain of her company?

'Okay, what did he do?' Kiki demanded, slamming her handbag onto the reception counter. The baby strapped to her front giggled and waved her arms and legs excitedly. 'Tell me everything—no matter how bad.'

Startled, Ruby gasped. 'Sorry…?'

'Don't make excuses for him—tell me. Your expression indicates it's pretty mega. Seriously, I've heard it all. You won't shock me.'

'Well, he asked me out to dinner.' The words escaped before Ruby could think better of saying them.

'What?' Kiki gasped.

'Dinner,' Ruby repeated, reaching out to stroke baby Neeve's hand. 'To eat.'

Looking as if she was on the verge of either crying or killing someone, Kiki demanded, '*Alex* asked you out to dinner?'

'Alex?' Ruby repeated, not sure what he had to do with their conversation.

'Yes,' Kiki nodded. 'Your boss—*my husband*! The man I gave my *heart* to.'

Ruby slowly shook her head. 'I haven't seen

Alex all morning. It wasn't *him* who asked me out to dinner.'

'Then who?'

Ruby stared at Kiki for several seconds, relieved to see the murderous expression had left the other woman's face. Then, licking her dry lips, she confessed, 'Kern.'

'Kern MacKinley?' Kiki cried, loud enough to startle her daughter and make her jump. 'Mr Gorgeous Racehorse Trainer?'

'Yes.'

'Not Alex?'

'No.' Ruby shook her head, not wanting to upset the woman again. 'He's always very kind to me, if a little abrupt. But he would never ask another woman out when he's so in love with you.'

'Those are his best qualities.' Kiki nodded, then grinned. 'In work hours, anyway.'

'Who are you talking about?' Anne asked as she joined them from one of the back rooms.

'Kern MacKinley,' Kiki answered. 'Our local hot and handsome celebrity.'

Anne sat on the chair behind the reception desk. 'Really? Tell all,' she demanded.

Kiki jumped in before Ruby could open her mouth. 'Ruby's going on a date with him.'

'Well...' Anne mused. 'I guess men who smell like horses do have their attractions.'

'He doesn't smell like horses,' Ruby argued, standing up for Kern.

He smelt like sunshine and hard work. Perhaps laughter, cuddles and river water. And if there was a slight horsey whiff to him occasionally, then it added to all the rest in a positive and manly way.

'He's more stallion—all muscle and horny!' Kiki giggled, then frowned. 'So why do you look pensive?'

'Because I have a date,' Ruby repeated, not sure why she'd decided to share with the other two women. She didn't normally gossip or open up about her feelings, but the urge to tell someone had proved irresistible. Though now she was seeing it might not have been one of her best ideas...

Kiki scrubbed at a stain on her daughter's sleeve. 'Why aren't you doing star jumps and cartwheels?' she asked. 'The man's yummy.'

'He's also a client,' Ruby reminded them.

Kiki waved an unconcerned hand. 'Oh, don't

worry about it. It's not a no-no for us. Go on the date and enjoy it.'

'But—'

All her doubts returned, stronger than ever. Was it a mistake to consider going out with Kern? Especially as he'd been forced into doing it. Why exactly had he asked her when he obviously hadn't wanted to? Was he really fed up with eating alone?

'But what?' Anne asked gently. 'Don't you like him? If you want to say no, you can. Tell him it's against the rules.'

Ruby dragged a hand through her curls and sighed. 'But Kiki just said it isn't.'

Her boss's wife piped up. 'That's when I thought you were eager to go.'

'I am. It's just...' Ruby hesitated, not sure how to explain the strange see-saw of emotions that had plagued her since she'd agreed to go. She didn't understand it herself.

'You're worried he might be a breast-grabber, aren't you?' Anne asked. 'Or perhaps a bum-toucher?'

'Yuck!' Kiki groaned, pulling a face at the older woman. 'What sort of men did you used to date?'

'Men who soon learnt to stop doing both after trying!' Anne chuckled.

Ruby shook her head, eager to dissuade the pair of that kind of idea. 'Kern's a gentleman.'

Kiki's eyes narrowed. 'You've already spent time with him, haven't you?'

Heat rose up Ruby's neck and over her face, giving her away. Why had she opened her big mouth? Kiki could give terriers and beagles lessons in sniffing out information.

'I checked his horse over one night and—'

'You've been moonlighting!' Kiki accused her. 'Wait until I tell Alex!'

Worried that she might lose her job, Ruby begged, 'Please don't.'

'But I must,' Kiki insisted. 'We've a bet going that Kern MacKinley fancies you, and I intend to win it. I plan to buy six hens with my winnings.'

'You do?' Ruby gasped, not certain she liked the idea of her non-existent love-life being gambled on.

The woman nodded, not in the least repentant at the discovery of her sneaky carry-on.

Ruby blushed once again, wishing she'd kept quiet. What would Kern think if he heard they had discussed him in this way? If the gossip reached his ears, would he think she had instigated it? Telling others that their friendship was more than casual.

'But he doesn't fancy me.'

'Did he ask you out to dinner?' Kiki probed.

'Yes.'

'There you go. He fancies you. That's how it started for Alex and I. Attraction over carrot soup and fresh bread. Next thing, he's asking to kiss me. It doesn't take much to get my man to pucker up.'

'But—but Eloise sort of pushed him into doing it,' Ruby stammered, then gave up.

Kern did not fancy her. He'd asked her out because he was too kind to come out and say he didn't want to. Probably believed he was saving her feelings.

Kiki snorted. 'From what I've seen of your Mr MacKinley, I doubt he lets anyone push him around.'

'Eloise is very forceful—and I think he feels guilty for staying away so long.'

Anne leaned back in her chair. 'Do you like him?'

Deciding to be honest, Ruby nodded. 'Yes,

I think I do—but not in a romantic way. As a friend.'

'Nothing wrong with friendship,' Anne agreed.

'Are you sure?' Kiki asked, sounding disappointed. 'Where's he taking you?'

'No idea,' Ruby admitted.

'You'll need smart but casual wear, then. With some thought I think we can turn your unique style into serious Goth class. You've the confidence to pull it off already.'

Ruby's heart twisted at the other woman's words. If only they were true. Sometimes she felt like the weakest person in the world.

'Let's go shopping in our dinner hour,' Kiki suggested.

Half afraid of the wild twinkle in Kiki's eyes, Ruby searched for a reason to decline.

'Good idea,' Anne encouraged. 'There's a new shop opened at the other end of the high street. Lots of velvet and lace. Just Ruby's sort of thing.'

'Perfect,' Kiki said. 'Don't worry—my taste is excellent. I married Alex, after all.'

For some reason Ruby didn't find that assurance truly comforting...

CHAPTER EIGHT

RUBY GLANCED DOWN at the simple black dress, with a small slit on one side, and muttered a prayer of hope that she wasn't overdressed. She'd teamed it with her mother's velvet jacket and simple silver jewellery. Velvet boots with a crisscross pattern gave her the perfect height, and she'd applied her make-up a little more heavily, coating her eyes and lips in a dark plum shade to match the small handbag she carried.

Standing outside the stables, where Kern had set up a temporary home, she fought the urge to rush inside, cancel, then leg it home.

The earlier shopping trip with Kiki had ended up being a mixture of both fun and embarrassment. The shop she'd dragged Ruby to *did* cater for her taste, and stocked lovely clothes, but the unwanted accompanying pearls of dating wisdom from Kiki had had Ruby cringing in the changing room.

She appreciated Kiki's help and insight, but the trouble was she and Kern weren't dating. Nothing near, in fact. Tonight's dinner was just two people sharing a meal. It didn't mean more than company and conversation. Which was perfect. Brief, safe and easy.

Then why are you nervous?

'Because,' she whispered aloud, placing a hand on her stomach to stop the nerves darting up and down, 'it feels like a lot more than a meal shared by friends. And even though I know it's best to keep things simple between us, I'm still a little excited.'

Raising her hand, she hesitated for a second, then knocked on the stable office door.

It opened instantly. Kern stood in the space, dressed in a pair of black jeans and a smart black shirt.

He stared at her for several moments before declaring, 'You're beautiful.'

She blushed, ridiculously pleased by his compliment. Warm pleasure swirled through her veins, setting off her nerves again. Silent warnings stirred in her head once more, but she ignored them, too captivated by the man in front of her.

'Thank you.'

He nodded politely. 'You're welcome.'

She giggled then, unable to prevent herself. 'Sorry, but this feels very odd.'

'Why?'

She shrugged, not really sure. Going out for the evening with this man felt unreal. She was just a newly qualified vet and he was a famous racehorse trainer. His world involved horses, wild characters and money. Hers included sick animals, their body fluids and their worried owners.

'It just does. Let's be honest—you didn't really want to ask me out, did you?'

'No, I didn't want my aunt to arrange a date *for* me,' he corrected. 'She seems to think I require help.'

'And do you?'

'No, I can ask a woman out all by myself,' he said, and then did so. 'Ruby, do you fancy going out tonight? I'd really love you to say yes.'

She pretended to consider his question. 'Well, seeing as we're all dressed up and ready…'

Kern laughed, then narrowed his eyes. 'Now we need to change what you're feeling to a more positive emotion.'

'We do?' she asked.

He put out a hand to her. 'Oh, yeah. Give me your hand.'

'My hand?' she repeated, sounding like a confused parrot. She rubbed it against the side of her dress and waited for him to explain.

'Yes—the thing hanging at the end of your arm.'

She presented him with her hand and wiggled her fingers. 'This thing?'

'Yep, that's the one.' He held it and tugged her into the office, kicking the door shut behind them a second later. Not giving her time to speak, he lifted her hand and trailed a finger across the centre of her palm. 'Oh, lookie here...'

Another giggle left her, thanks to the tickling sensation of his touch. And another wash of pleasant shivers raced through her. 'What are you doing?'

'Reading your palm.'

'I thought it was your aunt who believed in all that stuff?'

He glanced up. 'I'm a man of many talents, Ruby. It's not just you and my aunt with undisclosed powers.'

She raised an eyebrow. 'So you're not simply a piggyback knight?'

'Keep that quiet, won't you? I'd hate to fight back an adoring public, all desperate to experience my special skills.' He studied her hand again. 'It says clearly here that you need to stop worrying about what's going to happen in the next few hours, because fun is coming your way.'

'Is someone else joining us, then?' she asked cheekily.

He glared at her. 'You deserve a second dunking in the river for such a cruel remark.'

'But you're not going to give me one.'

'No, not when you look so beautiful.'

His blue eyes held hers until warmth tickled the back of her neck and oozed over her skin.

Flustered at both his words and scrutiny, she forced herself to act detached. 'I only agreed to tonight as a way of getting back at you for throwing me in the river. I think it's right to be honest with you.'

'So it wasn't the idea of spending time enjoying my company that made you agree?' he asked. His lower lip curved slightly in a disappointed frown.

'God, no,' she dismissed, fighting another smile. 'The bonus of a meal I don't have to cook swung it for me.'

Snorting, Kern returned his attention to her hand. 'Well, right here it says—'

A knock on the office door stopped him from continuing.

Kern glared at the wooden panel and muttered, 'Who the hell is *that*?'

She glanced down at her hand. 'Can't you see the answer in my palm?'

'My talents are a touch weak right now,' he admitted.

'Poor you,' she teased. 'Perhaps it's someone with a remedy for your impotent skills. It sounds like you may need it.'

A second knock filled the air. They both turned to stare at the door, but neither moved.

After a couple of seconds Ruby asked, 'Aren't you going to answer?'

Kern didn't shift. 'I'd rather stay right here, holding your hand, while you continue to enjoy crushing my fragile self-esteem.'

She giggled. 'I must admit it is fun.'

After the third knock, Ruby pointed out, 'Whoever is out there is getting impatient.'

'Their problem, not ours,' he insisted. 'Ignore their rudeness. We didn't invite them, did we?'

Ruby tried to pull her hand from his. 'You should answer it.'

Kern sighed heavily, giving her hand a gentle squeeze before letting go. 'Fine—but if I do, we'll be late for the restaurant.'

'Restaurant?'

His expression turned scolding. 'You didn't think I was going to serve you fish and chips here, did you?'

'I like fish and chips,' she answered.

'I'll remember that for some time in the future,' he promised and opened the door to reveal a small blond man, wearing designer country clothes and a disgruntled expression. 'You must be mad if you believed your last option was to come here.'

Kern stepped away and let the man enter the room. 'It was my *only* option.'

'Because you're too stubborn to call a friend when you need one,' the man complained, slapping Kern on the shoulder. 'It's good to see you. It's been far too long.'

'You too, Jacob. But not right now. You'll

need to postpone telling me the reason why you're here, because I have plans tonight.'

'Thanks for the enthusiastic welcome.' The visitor glanced Ruby's way, then returned his attention to Kern. 'God, what a dump.'

Kern folded his arms across his chest. 'Cheers for your tactless opinion on my family property. I'll try not to take offence. I guess you want to stay?'

'Of course. I have a meeting in Lambourne tomorrow. Why pay out for a hotel room when I can bum a sofa off you?'

'I don't own a sofa. All I can offer is a stable full of straw.'

'Good enough. I'm sure I can manage for one night. Won't be the first time I've bedded down in a pile of straw—though usually I'm not alone.'

'Why *are* you here?' Kern demanded, not looking pleased to see his friend.

'Because I intend to talk some sense into your thick head. If you think I am going to let my best friend of sixteen years rot in Dorset, then you need some sense knocked into you.'

Feeling awkward, Ruby pointed to the open door. 'I think I'll go…'

'No, stay,' Kern insisted. 'We have plans for tonight.'

'Yes,' Jacob drawled. 'You two go. I'll stay here and stare at the brickwork. Buy me a pizza on your way home, though. I haven't eaten in hours. Too busy travelling here to see *you*.'

Ruby moved towards the door; the atmosphere was suddenly uncomfortable. 'No, you stay here with your friend. We can go out another night. I'm happy to postpone my revenge for a later day.'

Kern reached for her. 'But I'm not. Ruby— wait.'

She dodged his hand and after a second's hesitation placed a chaste kiss upon his cheek, desperately missing their flirtatious and jokey connection. His skin was rough and firm against her lips and she fought the urge to linger against it.

'Thanks for asking, anyway. Both times. Goodnight, Kern.'

Waving the men goodbye, she rushed from the office and headed back home to her empty caravan. Some things weren't meant to be, and going out to a restaurant with Kern MacKinley was obviously one of them. The man had friends from his past to help him. Did he really need her to clutter up his time? Someone with just as disillusioned a view on relationships and no real clue how to even be in one?

'What the hell are you thinking, returning to this backwater?' Jacob asked. 'Did you think I would let you scurry away and be forgotten? After everything you've done for me over the years? No trainer would have touched me in the early days without your faith in me. There's a few even now who'd think twice.'

Kern closed the door, wishing he could follow Ruby. The last thing he required right now was an evening listening to his friend harp on about the so-called mistakes he'd made. Not when all he wanted to do was rush after Ruby and convince her to stay and spend the evening with him.

'You like to win—there's no shame in that. The best jockeys do. You just need to learn to stay away from unsuitable women. Especially the ones married to trainers.'

'I'm ruthless. Unfortunately, you're too nice— otherwise you would have divorced Corinne years ago. Sorry about what happened with her, by the way.'

'Thanks, but don't start,' Kern warned, still furious at having to postpone his date.

Jacob had always had seriously rotten timing, but tonight was his worst offence. Hadn't he heard of phoning before arriving? Letting a person know he intended to visit?

'Besides, we've not spoken in over a year.'

Jacob shrugged. 'Had a bit of trouble in Argentina,' he admitted. 'Long story. But I met a man out there—a sheikh—and he's keen to start his own yard. When I heard what had happened to you, I suggested you become his trainer. Have all the fun while he foots all the bills. A perfect way to re-enter the game until you can afford to go out on your own again.'

'No.'

Kern refused even to consider the offer. It was one thing to deal with owners who thought they knew everything—another to be completely beholden to a rich man's whim.

'Just think for a minute,' Jacob urged.

Kern walked over to the chair behind the desk and sat down. 'I don't need to. It's not for me, thanks. I'm not even sure what my plans are yet.'

'Well, I hope they don't include the stable girl who just left?' Jacob remarked.

Kern stiffened, not liking Jacob's tone. It was one thing for Jacob to have an opinion of Corinne, because he had known her and their troubles, but he refused to let the man condemn a woman he'd not been polite enough even to acknowledge.

'Her name's Ruby and she's a local vet—not a stable girl.'

Jacob sighed. 'I'm here for one night and we need to talk over this opportunity properly. It's perfect for you. It's the ideal answer to your run of bad luck.'

'I can sort myself out. I don't need any help from rich playboys with too much money and too little care for the horses in their stables. All the man would focus on is the prize money and swanning around with royalty and the upper class. We'd soon fall out.'

'Wrong. The man admires you. And if you want more control over everything, I'm sure you can discuss it with him and come to an agreement which satisfies you both.'

Kern shook his head, keen to change the subject. 'Why don't I order that pizza?'

He pulled out his phone from his trouser pocket and searched for the number, though his appetite had diminished now he knew he wouldn't be sharing a meal with Ruby.

'So, the woman who just left…?' Jacob asked, settling on a stool. 'The vet?'

Kern gripped the phone and glanced up to find Jacob watching him. 'Ruby? What about her?'

'Anything serious?'

Kern returned his attention to his phone, flicking through the numbers without seeing them. Common sense dictated that he should halt anything serious from developing between him and Ruby, but he couldn't ignore the part of him that secretly yearned for it.

Regardless of his reservations about spending more time with her, and the underhand, sneaky way his aunt had manoeuvred them into tonight's date, he'd started to look forward to it. Had wanted to indulge in one night of her company just for the pleasure of it.

'No,' he said. 'We're friends. She cares for Enticing Evie.'

'Good,' Jacob said. 'I'd hate another woman to screw things up for you. Last thing you need is another heavy relationship.'

Kern turned away, his thoughts still focused on Ruby. Was she angry with him for not taking her out, or as disappointed as he was that they'd had to cancel? Or was she perhaps secretly relieved they'd had to abandon their date?

As much as he hated to admit it, Jacob was right about one important matter. A relationship was the last thing he should contemplate. He might be slowly piecing his life back into order, but he had nothing to offer any woman. No job, no savings—he didn't even live in a proper home. All he had was broken dreams, a tarnished reputation and run-down property. Hardly the stuff a woman dreamed of when searching for a man.

For Ruby's sake he needed to remember just how little he had to offer. He'd already disappointed one woman in his life. Decency determined that he not be selfish and make it two.

CHAPTER NINE

'HE'S LOOKING MUCH BETTER.' Kern crouched to rub Dog's head.

The Wolfhound wagged his tail in reply, but didn't move from the rug he and Ruby sat on beside the caravan. Ruby tried to dodge the frantic whipping of her pet's tail as he tried to crawl closer to their visitor in his desperation to lick his face.

She'd not seen or heard from Kern for three days. Not that she'd noticed his absence, thanks to work. And she certainly didn't daydream about him—much.

'Hey, Dog...' Kern continued to pet the large dog. 'Digging the shaved leg look you're sporting. Bet all the female pooches give you the canine love-eye. Handsome male like you.'

Ruby sniggered. 'I'm pretty sure a Labrador cross laughed at him when we left the practice on the day he came home.'

Kern shook his head in sympathy. 'That,

my friend, is women for you. Always ready to mock when we try our best. They're cruel to us poor, innocent males.'

'Huh!' Ruby scoffed. 'You're about as innocent as a sinner hanging out in hell. Is this a passing visit, or does your horse need my expertise again?'

'No, Evie and Mabel Star—'

'*Mabel* Star?' she asked.

'My aunt's renamed her horse Mabel Star after some past ancestor she reminds Eloise of. It's the ears, apparently.'

Ruby shook her head. 'I see...'

'The actual reason for my visit is that it's a beautiful day and I thought you might like to go to the beach with me.'

Ignoring the sudden leap in her stomach, Ruby glanced at her dog with his fresh dressing, knowing she had no choice but to refuse. 'Dog's not really able to walk along the beach with his leg the way it is.'

'My aunt has insisted Dog stays with her for the day,' Kern explained quickly. 'There's a rerun of a murder mystery series she wants to watch on TV, and she figures Dog will enjoy watching it with her.'

Ruby hesitated, torn between staying at home with her pet and going to the seaside with Kern. On such a nice day, the thought of spending time lazing around on the sand sounded wonderful.

'I'd hate to take advantage of Eloise...'

'Sometimes it's good to,' Kern murmured, kneeling on the rug to rub Dog's stomach.

Ruby envied the way Kern's fingers ran back and forth over her pet. How would it feel if the man touched *her* in such an informal and intimate way?

Leaning back on her arms, Ruby forced herself to focus, and stop contemplating irrelevant questions she would never learn the answers to. 'It is?'

He nodded. 'You never know what might happen when you grasp the advantage—what surprises you might discover by doing so.'

Ruby narrowed her eyes, suspicious of his deep, persuading tone. 'Why do I suspect there's more to your invitation than just a trip to the seaside?'

He glanced up and chuckled. 'Because I haven't told you everything and you're a very smart woman.'

She crossed her ankles. 'I've found it best to be smart where you're concerned, Kern MacKinley.'

He sat on his heels and held up his hands in defeat. 'Okay, I'll confess. There's a horse I've arranged to look at and I thought you might like to join me.'

'A racehorse?' she asked curiously. That made more sense than a sudden urge to go paddling in the sea. Did his friend Jacob have anything to do with it?

'Does this have something to do with your friend's visit the other night?'

Kern shook his head. 'No, Jacob called in for another reason. Someone Eloise knows has tipped her off about a colt being a good buy. And to stop her nagging I've agreed to go and check it out. I'm considering him—nothing more.'

'And you'd like my expert eye?' she asked, wondering what his friend had wanted.

'I'd love your company, and although my eye is as expert as yours when it comes to horse-flesh,' he replied easily, 'a medical judgement is always welcome.'

'Really? Maybe we should compare notes

and see which one of us has the more intensive equine knowledge?'

Kern's gaze didn't shift from hers. 'I'd love to. Perhaps we can reschedule our dinner date?'

'Sounds possible,' she said, her heart racing at his closeness and at his offer. 'You do realise I should charge you for my expert opinion?'

'Dinner not payment enough?'

'Oh, no. That's payback for dumping me in the river,' she reminded him. 'Perhaps I should add interest, seeing as you cancelled.'

'How about I buy you an ice cream?'

'Done,' she agreed.

He stood and stared down at her. 'Eloise will enjoy spoiling Dog and talking his ear off. He'll be the perfect guest. He doesn't answer back or argue with her opinion.'

'You make a convincing argument,' she said, gazing at him.

'Then say yes. You want to. I can tell. And you're already dressed for it,' he said, taking in her dark leggings and black T-shirt.

'If you're sure Eloise doesn't mind?' she asked, worried the old lady might.

'She doesn't,' he assured her. 'You can ask

her when we drop Dog off and pick up the basket of food she's preparing for us.'

'A picnic?' she quizzed, delighted at the thought. 'You were that confident I would agree?'

He grinned and reached to help her up. 'No. But Eloise was.'

Ruby stepped onto the soft sand ahead of the man who'd driven them to the secluded cove. The drive in his old horsebox had stirred unsettling memories, but Kern's constant chatter had stopped Ruby from dwelling on them for too long.

Breathing in the crisp, fresh, salty air, she took in the cerulean blue sky, broken only by a distant faint white line of cloud where Nature had dragged her artistic finger lightly across the horizon in a lax attempt to define between the sea and sky.

Turning from the beautiful scenery, she pushed away a curl from where it dangled in her eyes, thanks to the light warm breeze coming off the water, and asked, 'I thought we were seeing the horse first?'

The same breeze ran invisible fingers through

Kern's hair, too. Light and playful, like a lover's caressing touch, ruffling the thick dark strands and causing Ruby's own fingers to want to follow their curious path.

How would his hair feel against her palms? Soft? Wiry? Perfect for tugging playfully when he kissed her?

Kissed her?

She swallowed and turned to the sea again, her mind suddenly confused and muddled. Playful tugging? Kissing? What was she thinking? Nothing like that would transpire between them, so it didn't matter what his hair felt like. He was a friend, and friends did not touch each other's hair. No matter how much they might wish to.

'We are,' Kern answered, his eyes sparkling with a trace of secrecy.

The breeze blew his green T-shirt against his body, outlining the muscles beneath, and the black tight-fitting jodhpurs that encased his firm legs created a truly mouth-watering sight. Kern MacKinley was one attractive man.

Not sure what he meant, Ruby continued to stare towards the expanse of deep blue water. The last time she'd visited a beach there'd been ice creams and buckets and spades for sale. The odd donkey might have hung around, but she'd never seen a racehorse.

'I don't understand,' she said, tilting her head to one side.

She was intrigued by Kern's expression and the mischievous twinkle lightening his eyes. Once again, the sensation that he was up to something raised her curiosity.

Kern rested an arm across her shoulders, immediately enclosing her with his body heat and aftershave. Spicy and light, she liked it. She also rather enjoyed feeling his arm around her.

'The horse's owner recommended we meet him here,' he said. 'This is a private beach that belongs to his family. What do you say? Fancy a ride along the sand?'

Her distraction at his close presence vanished instantly. Working with horses was one thing, but she avoided occasions for actually riding one where possible. Others carried out the riding and she concentrated on the diagnosing. Just the idea of riding for pleasure alone evoked more memories from her childhood, and not all of them good.

'I'm not sure...'

Kern frowned down at her. 'I didn't think to ask. Can you ride?'

She nodded, then admitted, 'It's been a while, though.'

Relief chased his frown away and he tugged her closer. 'What better location to start again? Come on—say yes. I promise a soft landing if you fall off.'

Insulted at the idea, she snorted. 'I'm sure I can remember how to stay on, thank you.'

She focused her eyes on the gentle sea foam ripples intimately caressing the sand.

Just her and Kern.

Until the owner and the horses arrived.

'It's beautiful here,' she whispered.

The words were whipped away on the wind. But Kern must have caught them, because he answered. 'Yes, it is. Truly stunning. Will you ride with me, Ruby? I promise to lend you some sun cream if you do.'

With lingering reluctance, she nodded, and then smiled when he produced a bottle from his back pocket. 'See—I'm a man of his word and always prepared.'

She laughed and took the sun cream from him. Kern made her want to do things she normally avoided. All the things she'd purposely denied herself for years.

What would her parents think about her reluctance to do something she'd loved as a child? One of the few things they'd jointly encouraged her to pursue? Would they be horrified that she had taken a different path involving horses, tending to their physical care and well-being, and not the one they'd hoped she would aim for in the show ring? Or would they feel pride that not only had she worked hard to reach her goals, but she was now following her dream career?

'The horses are here,' Kern said.

He grabbed her hand and pulled her towards a man walking along the water's edge with two thoroughbred horses. One grey and one bay. Their coats gleamed in the sunshine.

'Good morning.' Kern shook the man's hand and they chatted for several minutes about the horses' general health and personalities.

Ruby moved closer to the bay horse, offering her hand under its nose.

Kern finished quizzing the owner and asked, 'Need a leg-up?'

She nodded, suddenly shaky. What if she'd

forgotten everything her parents had taught her? What if all those riding lessons deserted her and left her bouncing and jigging along like a half-terrified novice? 'Thanks.'

'Ready?' Kern asked, only a second before he grabbed her leg and pushed her upwards.

The strangeness of sitting on a horse after so long hit Ruby hard the moment her bottom settled on the leather saddle. But, like an old pro, she reached for the reins and wrapped them correctly around her fingers. Relieved that she remembered the basics, at least, she waited for Kern to adjust the stirrups, concentrating on slowing her breathing, not wanting the bay to sense her nerves.

Kern mounted the other horse, and with a quick goodbye to the owner they slowly headed along the wet sand, leaving deep hoofprints in their wake.

For several minutes neither spoke, content to let the horses splash through the water. Seagulls squalled above and sunlight reflected from the sea as though crushed glass floated upon the waves.

Halfway along the cove, Kern nudged his

horse closer to hers so they could ride side by side. 'Having fun?' he asked.

Ruby couldn't deny it. Everything about this was perfect. The horse, the surroundings and the man. Especially the man.

'What do you think of him?' she asked, nodding towards the grey. By sight alone she couldn't detect any obvious physical issues in his movements or appearance.

'He's nice to handle. Definitely has potential. But he's going to cost a good chunk of my money. I'll be eating crackers and cheese for the next few months if I decide to buy him. How's yours?'

'Wonderful. Is he very expensive?'

'No. Between us, he's ridiculously cheap. But it's still a lot of money to risk when I'm counting every pound,' Kern mused.

'Too much of a risk, then?'

He glanced at her. 'Life's a risk, Ruby. But it's also a reason to get up in the morning.'

'Why's the owner selling?' she asked. If the horse was sound, why didn't the owner want to keep him?

'The man has an interest in several horses already,' Kern answered. 'He wants to offload this one because his trainer doesn't think he has the talent or skill to compete against the best.'

The glimmer in Kern's eyes said differently.

'What do *you* think?' Ruby asked, curious to know how he viewed the horses. What did a racehorse trainer search for in an animal? Was it purely physical? Or was there more to it than just speed?

'I think with time, proper training and a good dose of luck, this horse has a chance to win some big races. He has talent. It's his trainer who doesn't. I found several recordings of his previous races on the internet last night, and instinct tells me there's more to this horse than he's shown.'

'Sounds like you're going to buy him. Does this mean you intend to start training again?'

Kern shrugged. 'I can do some work with him and sell him on later if I need to. I lost my yard because people stopped trusting me with their horses after the fire. It's hard to come back from a knock like that. I'm not sure I have the drive to do it again, you know?'

In a way, she did. For a long time she'd lived each day with no aim other than to get through it without thinking of her parents and the past.

But when she'd decided to become a vet it had given her a purpose, a challenge. A reason to get out of bed, to use her brain, and to indulge her love of creatures who required her help and care.

Animals had never left her feeling emotionally bruised and drained, as her parents often had after one of their many confrontations.

'You've a good seat,' said Kern. 'Who taught you to ride?'

Ruby licked the salt from her lips and answered, 'My parents.'

Kern stared intently at her. 'Why do I get the feeling you're the one holding secrets now?'

She shook her head, and they continued to the end of the cove and then slowly headed back again. Even though Ruby was concentrating on her horse, she sensed Kern glancing at her several times. Was he wondering about her parents? Or perhaps wondering why she didn't ride any more?

When they returned to where the owner waited, the man directed them to the path leading to his farm and stables. There, the next forty-five minutes consisted of both Ruby and Kern giving the grey colt a thorough check-over. After haggling over the price, Kern shook the owner's hand and worked out the arrangements to collect the horse the following day.

'So you own another horse?' she said as they left the yard.

'I do,' Kern said, opening a wooden gate that led back down to the cove.

'Are you sure you haven't come to a decision about your future?' she asked.

For someone who professed not to know, he was committing both time and money to staying at MacKinley farm. And what about his friend Jacob? The few minutes' conversation she'd witnessed had made it clear the man considered Kern mad for coming back.

He shook his head and swung the gate shut. 'No, not yet. But as I said before, I can resell the colt for a profit once I've done some work with him.'

'Why *did* you return to Dorset?' Ruby asked.

What had called him back to the place he'd apparently avoided for years? After making a life elsewhere, why return to the place he'd run from?

'Honestly?' he asked. 'I had nowhere else to take Evie and very little money to keep us both. Desperation brought me home—and a deep need to see my aunt. I've neglected Eloise for far too long. I realised I'd tried to recreate what was here somewhere else, but the truth is, there's only one MacKinley farm. How crazy is that? It took losing what I thought was important to realise that fact.'

'What now?' Ruby asked, pleasantly relaxed despite the slight ache in her thighs, as they wandered back to the beach.

Being on horseback had reminded her of how much she missed it. She didn't want to compete, the way she had as a child, but now the occasional ride might be fun.

Kern shrugged. 'I thought we'd eat our picnic on the beach before returning home. The owner said we could.'

'Sounds nice, but Dog—'

'Is with my aunt—and she prepared the picnic, remember?' he soothed. 'She's trying to matchmake, you know?'

Ruby nodded, suddenly awkward. 'Does it bother you?'

He didn't answer. Instead, he urged, 'Find a nice spot for us to sit and I'll fetch the basket from the van. I hope she's fixed something tasty. I'm starving.'

Ruby grinned as they parted and went in different directions. 'Me too.'

Though she doubted food would satisfy the huge hunger developing deep inside her every time she and Kern spent time alone together.

'Egg sandwiches!' Ruby declared, unwrapping the foil covering the first package she'd retrieved from the old-fashioned wicker basket.

Kern reached over and swiped a sandwich from the pile. 'Great. My favourite.'

She held the rest out of his reach and nodded towards the basket. 'See what else is in there.'

He withdrew two crisp packets, chocolate bars, fizzy drinks and finally a large pork pie. Holding it up, he went to take a bite, but Ruby whipped it out of his hand before his lips touched the pastry and put it in her own mouth.

'Hey!' he yelled.

Munching a large mouthful, she grinned at his shocked expression, and then took another ravenous bite of the pie. 'Sorry, but I'm starving. Blame the sea air.'

'So am I,' he said, helping himself to another

sandwich before she prevented him. 'I never suspected you were a food stealer.'

'It's a bad habit,' she joked. 'I try to resist, but occasionally the urge is too much for me to fight.'

He finished his sandwich and then reached for another. This time she shared without any fuss.

'Can I ask you a question?' he asked.

Wary of his serious tone, she mused, 'Is it personal or professional?'

'Personal.'

She continued chewing her pilfered pie, not sure she wanted the pleasant moment ruined. 'Very personal or a little bit personal?'

'Very,' he answered.

Licking grease from her fingertips, she shrugged. 'Okay. What do you want to know? Though you can only ask one question.'

He leaned back on one elbow and smiled. 'Is this revenge for the other day?'

Ruby nodded, and quoted his words back to him. 'I like the odds to be in my favour. Come on—ask your question so I can get on with stealing more of your food.'

'Did you never learn to share as a child?' he quizzed, tapping her on the nose.

'Nope. Only child.'

'Yeah, me too. But I always share when needed.'

She laughed, not the least bit bothered by his criticism. Taking his food before he could eat it made her happy. Or rather the shocked expression on his face did. A little friendly teasing lifted a heavy soul, and she suspected Kern's was pretty weighty.

'And I appreciate it. The pie was delicious.'

He glared at her for a moment, then asked, 'How long ago did you start wearing Goth make-up?'

Surprised, she considered not answering. But Kern had shared his past with her the other night, so would it really hurt to tell him a little of her own? She wasn't confessing the secrets of her heart—not the deeply hidden ones that lingered among the doubts. Just a small snippet of data.

'When I was sixteen,' she said, reaching for a bottle of drink. She twisted open the lid, but didn't drink from it.

'Do you wear it to hide the scar on your neck?'

His second question threw her completely. She rested the bottle in her lap and asked, 'You've seen it?'

'Yes—the day I threw you into the river. Patches of your make-up washed off and exposed it.'

She fiddled with the bottle's lid. Twisting it on and off. 'Why didn't you ask then?'

'I figured you'd tell me if it mattered. I'm more curious about the make-up.'

Ruby pondered his words, then sighed heavily. Most people would regard her scar as more interesting, but Kern wasn't like other people. Was that because of his own scars? The ones on his heart because of his marriage? Whenever he spoke of his wife, guilt and regret shaded his words. Was he not asking about the scar because he respected the fact that everyone had scars that were often best left alone?

'Don't you like my make-up?' she asked. 'Does it offend you?'

Kern shook his head. 'No, I'm just curious. It seems to clash with your personality.'

She frowned at him. 'What do you mean?'

'You're beautiful, but shy, and yet you wear make-up which causes people to notice you.

Two forces at odds, surely? Who's the real Ruby?'

'I'm not beautiful,' she denied, uncomfortable with his comment.

'Yes, you are,' he insisted, touching her cheek. 'You're very beautiful—and your scar does nothing to detract from it.'

Disturbed by his touch, she blurted, 'I wear it as camouflage. To stop people from recognising my face.'

Why had she said that? Why not tell the man that she loved the Goth look and leave it at that? What had happened to sharing only a vague morsel of information?

His expression tightened as he absorbed her words. 'Are you famous?'

She'd put herself in this hole—now she had to find a way out without confessing more. 'No, not me. My parents were well-known. The scar is from where a bullet grazed my skin. It happened a long time ago. It's nothing.'

Kern's intense gaze didn't flinch. The slight tightening of his fingers against the curve of her skin was his only reaction to her statement. 'Who did it?'

Great. She'd hoped by acting as though it was

nothing he'd stop asking questions. Trust Kern to do the opposite.

Gripping the bottle, she whispered, 'My father.'

'Why?'

She sighed. 'He wanted to stop the guilt that consumed him every time he stared at my face and saw my mother's instead.'

'Your mother?'

'Chantel Dainnes,' she said, releasing the name from the secret part of her heart where she'd suppressed it for so long, desperate to keep their connection hidden.

'The French model?' Kern questioned.

She nodded. 'When I wear the Goth make-up I don't resemble her as much. It's enough to stop people from making a connection between us.'

'I see,' Kern replied. He lowered his hand and grasped her own. His gaze searched hers as he shuffled the pieces into sense. 'So Frank Day, the jockey, was your father?'

Ruby sucked in a deep breath, then released it slowly. 'Yes.'

'But didn't he go to jail for trying to shoot

his daughter—?' His words dried up. 'Oh, my God. He tried to *kill* you.'

She nodded and drew her knees up to rest her arms on them. Why not tell Kern the rest and give him the truth, instead of risking him searching on the internet, where lies and hearsay waited for the gullible to read and believe? Because of her big mouth, there wasn't any other choice.

'My parents' marriage was stormy. One week they loved each other—the next they hated one another. My father was critical, bad-tempered and controlling. Mostly because he battled hunger daily, trying to retain his weight for riding. Whereas my mother represented beauty to the world, but around my father she became ugly. She made him feel inadequate and small— literally. They were two people who purposely enjoyed wounding each other and thrived on doing it often. Together they played games of spite and point-scoring. They were each other's poison and they never should have married. But to the world they pretended to be faithful and in love. The perfect couple.'

'And *you* were stuck in the middle of that?'

She nodded. 'Oh, they loved me—but each

other…? Well, it depended on their mood. One day my mother left home to go on a photoshoot, but returned to the house when she became ill. She searched for my father and found him with the housekeeper, doing the one thing she refused to forgive. She'd endure the fights, the drinking and the gambling, but adultery was her limit.'

Kern reached out and drew her down beside him and into his arms, sheltering her from the wind coming off the sea and the shadows floating up from the past.

Ruby closed her eyes for a second, savouring the closeness.

'She left the house with me in tow, after threatening to drag my father through the courts and destroy him. She drove to my father's agent's house and left me there. Then she travelled to our London apartment and swallowed a ton of pills to numb the pain permanently.'

Kern's hold tightened around her. 'What happened afterwards?'

'I returned to live with my father for a few weeks, but every time we were together he'd cry and yell. He'd talk to me as though I was my mother. Begging, pleading for forgiveness. The one thing I was unable to give because I wasn't my mother. Plus, I *didn't* forgive him. The housekeeper wasn't his first affair—just the first my mother discovered. I knew there'd been others before. His grief and guilt sent him crazy and his behaviour became erratic.'

'Oh, Ruby...'

'One day I was in the stables, seeing to our horses because no one else bothered, when my father appeared with his handgun and turned it on me.'

'You must have been terrified.'

She nodded and gripped Kern's arms, finding the strength to continue through touching him. 'Fortunately, my father's agent turned up unexpectedly, and shoved my father backwards as he took aim. The bullet grazed my chin and neck, leaving me with this scar, but alive.'

'Thank goodness...'

'He called an ambulance and the police while my father wept on the floor. Later my father confessed that he'd planned to turn the gun on himself afterwards, because he wanted us to join my mother. They'd barely managed to live together in life, and yet he couldn't live without her once she was gone.'

'What happened then?'

'My father's agent offered me a home. With no other family, I accepted. I'd known him for most of my life. He supported me through the court case. Stood by me when the newspapers villainised my mother and I—'

'You?'

She glanced at him wearily. 'They wanted someone to rip apart, and I was the only one they could get to. I'd lost all my friends, and hardly left the house. The few times I did, I was followed and offered money to spill secrets about my parents. And then there were my mother's and my father's fans, who accused me of lying because they didn't want to believe they'd fallen so easily for my father's great guy persona and my mother's perfect image. It all became horrendous and suffocating.'

'Oh, Ruby,' he soothed.

'A few months later, although I'd thought I could trust my father's agent, he sold the story of my parents' marriage to those same newspapers. Sold the secrets I'd confided in him because I thought he cared and it was safe.'

Kern kissed the side of her face. 'The man abused your trust. You were a child who needed his protection.'

'That's when I used the Goth make-up for the first time. One day I packed a bag and left the house for good. I walked down the street for the first time in months and no one recognised me.'

Kern cupped her cheek with his hand and gently drew her face to his. 'What a crap hand they dealt you.'

She wrinkled her nose. 'Not a great one, I guess. But plenty of people deal with worse. I managed, and my life is pretty good. I transferred to a different school, moved on to university, then decided to train as a vet. The best decision of my life.'

'Beautiful and brave.'

She squirmed with embarrassment. 'I just did what I had to. One thing my mother did teach me was that if I wanted something or needed something then I should work for it. So I did.'

'You must hate horse racing and everything about it.'

She shook her head. 'No, I don't. My parents' relationship was troubled because of who they were—not what they did. Everything they did together was destructive, yet they couldn't face being without each other.'

'Not everything,' he said. 'They made you.'

'There's something else you should know,' she confessed, deciding to clear her conscience completely.

'Yes?'

'I can heal animals,' she said. She hated not being honest about her gift, and Kern already had suspicions about what had occurred when he'd left the stables the night she'd tended to Evie. 'What I mean is, I help animals in pain, emotionally and physically, by placing my hands on them.'

Kern gazed at her silently, then grinned. 'You're a healer?'

She tensed. 'Yes.'

He continued to stare down at her, his expression thoughtful. 'Are you saying you put your hands on Evie and made her better? I've heard and read about people who can, but I've never known anyone who actually does it.'

'Do you think I'm a freak?' she blurted out, worried he would see her differently now. People tended to when she admitted to being able to do something unusual. And, despite her trying to keep this man as a mere friend, she knew his opinion mattered to her. It shouldn't, but it did.

'No,' he soothed, softly stroking the outline of her lower lip with his thumb. 'I think you're special and talented and I really want to kiss you.'

She blinked up at him. She could see the tiny bristles over his face and feel the warm breath coming from his lips. 'You do?'

'Yes.'

'But wouldn't that be a terrible idea, considering we're only friends?' she asked, licking her lower lip.

'Yes,' he agreed. 'I haven't wanted to kiss a woman in such a long time, but I can't help wondering how your lips will feel under my own.'

'I keep speculating about what your hair feels like,' she admitted.

He leaned closer and encouraged her. 'Why don't you touch it and satisfy your curiosity.'

She clenched her hands to stop herself from giving in to his appealing invitation. 'But as friends we're not allowed to touch each other in any caressing way. It's a rule.'

'I'm not one for rules...'

She tilted her head farther back and looked him straight in the eye. 'So why don't you break it, then?'

CHAPTER TEN

RUBY LICKED HER LIPS, her breath caught somewhere between racing and suspended in a strange elevation of time, sensation and hope. Would he or wouldn't he?

Did he dare lean forward those last few inches that separated them and place his lips against hers? Kiss her until her thoughts vanished and her nerve ends tingled?

Did she dare kiss him?

Her mouth dried at the thought of kissing Kern. Would he taste the way he did in her dreams? The erotic ones that plagued her in the dark night and left her hot and achy? The dreams she loved to disappear into, knowing he was there with her, doing things she'd never done with anybody else.

He sighed after a moment. 'You're too young for me,' he said.

The logical words sliced through the humming daze of her craving with icy cold reality.

Too young? What did age have to do with this and the way he made her feel? Did age cause her to tremble and simmer with heat until she yearned to douse herself with cold water for some relief? Age didn't make her laugh after a hard day, or offer the comforting safety of his arms. Age had nothing to do with this strange attraction building between them. Age wasn't a concern and he'd no business using it as an excuse.

She smiled and touched his face, slipping her fingers lightly over his rough skin. He needed a shave, but she liked this shadowy appearance on him. It suited his rough-around-the-edges personality. No, she was lying. She *loved* it.

'Why am I too young?' she asked, not about to let him off without explaining. She understood his cautiousness, because of his past, but was he using their age difference as a reason or an excuse?

'I don't mean in age,' he said. 'I mean in life's hardships. You're innocent, sweet and pure, and I am old and cynical. You deserve someone who's not beaten and—'

'Did I not just tell you about my parents?' she asked, curious as to why he perceived her life as being spotless compared to his own when he knew better.

'But you haven't let your circumstances harden you. Your heart is still soft and—'

'That's not true,' she argued. 'I struggle to be myself around people and I'm always worried they'll find out the truth about who my parents are.'

'Would that be so bad?' he quizzed.

'Yes,' she said. 'People loved my parents—or at least they loved the fake image they showed the world. When the truth came out, the public reacted as though it was all my fault. Because I looked like my mother, they blamed me for what my father did. It was twisted and horrible and it didn't make any sense. And it didn't help that my father refused to accept that he'd tried to kill me or that his actions drove my mother to suicide. Do you really think I want to rake all that up again and have it taint what I have now? For the first time in my life I have people who accept me. Work colleagues who treat me as one of the team. I have real friends.'

'And I'm included in those friends?' Kern asked, touching her face again.

She nodded. 'I hope so.'

His hand stilled and he sighed. 'Giving in to this attraction between us is a bad idea.'

'Why?'

'Because I see hope glimmering in your eyes, sweetheart. Do you honestly see any in mine?'

She rested her finger against his lips and smiled softly. No, she didn't see hope. She saw disappointment and pain and so much regret. But she didn't care, because none of those emotions was to do with *her*. What they had was new and clean.

'I like you as you are, Kern. Battered or not. Just shut up and kiss me, won't you? Am I asking you for anything else?'

'But you won't find me attractive for long,' he argued. 'I might infect you with my bad luck. My track record concerning relationships is poor—'

'Maybe I'll melt your bad luck away and replace it with some good,' she interrupted.

Right now, she sought only to try. Everything about this man caused her to wish for more than she'd ever had before. Perhaps hope did still linger in her heart. She certainly longed for his kiss…

'Spending time with you would change any

man for the better,' said Kern, slipping his hand into her hair. His blue eyes were thoughtful and serious as he studied her face. 'You're beautiful.'

She wasn't, but under his gaze she felt it. When he looked at her he saw not a Goth or a vet but Ruby. No one had ever observed her with such intensity and need. Not just casual lust, but more a curious hungry desire. As though he craved to consume her slowly. The way a person relished a delicious sweet mouthful they knew they shouldn't indulge in.

'Are you going to kiss me or not?' she asked brazenly, impatient for him to do so. Forget talking—she required full-on lip engagement.

His fingers tightened against her scalp. 'I should finish off those sandwiches…'

She winced. 'Not only too young, but second to your appetite? Man, you're battering my self-worth here, with such unromantic declarations.'

'Is that what you want, Ruby?' he asked, his eyes twinkling. 'Romantic words and verses? I'm not sure I'll be any good at that stuff.'

'No, I want you to kiss me. The rest's not necessary—unless you really want to show me your inner poet. Though, to be honest, poetry kind of bores me.'

'I'm tempted to try,' he said, slowly pushing her backwards until she sank into the soft grains of sand. 'I want to kiss you much more than I want to eat, I swear, but if I kiss you once I'm going to want to put another kiss here on your cheek, and then there on your neck, and perhaps one—'

'Sounds perfect,' she encouraged, melting into the swirling layers of his voice and the shivers that danced like plumes across her skin.

Everything about Kern intrigued her. His looks, his voice… He excited her and scared her. An irresistible combination. She wanted to grab him close and ignore the fear of getting hurt. Wanted him to be the one man she could truly trust and know he would never break that trust.

'Are you nervous?' Kern asked, his tone serious as he studied her face. 'I promise my kiss won't hurt.'

'It's afterwards I'm worried about,' she admitted, brushing his hair back from his forehead. It was soft and thick, exactly the way she'd imagined it.

'Well, if you hate the kiss you can slap my face and wash out your mouth with some lemonade. I promise not to be offended.'

'It's not th-that,' she stammered, unsure how to explain.

She desired his kiss—she really did—but what happened after? Another kiss or three? More than just kisses? Would he want to make love to her here on the beach? In public?'

'Tell me,' he coaxed.

Taking hold of her courage, she did. 'What are you hoping will happen *after* the kiss?'

Comprehension softened his features and a faint smile teased his lips. 'Ruby, if we make love I promise we'll be doing it somewhere private and comfortable, with no risk of a passing gull using my naked butt as target practice. As I'm sure you know, animal mess is no fun.'

She giggled and relaxed. 'In that case, Mr MacKinley, stop being concerned with all the reasons not to, and get on with kissing me.'

He hesitated, as though he still sensed her wariness. 'It's only a kiss. And only if you like it will I do it again. You're in control of what happens.' He rested his forehead against her own. 'Trust me. I know what I'm doing.'

She wrinkled her nose and voiced her last remaining doubt. 'What if you hate kissing *me*?'

He rubbed a soothing thumb over her chin. 'I suspect you're going to be the best kisser who's ever walked this earth. And do you know why?'

'Why?'

'Because this is you and I, and there's strong chemistry between us. It's special and rare.'

'There is?' she asked shyly. His words were reassurance against the last threads of her insecurity.

He nodded. 'Kiss me, Ruby. Throw a spell over me the way you did my horse. Use your magic hands on me, darling.'

He kissed her then, using his hand on the back of her head to draw her deeper into his embrace. His mouth was warm and persuasive as their breath joined and their tongues met for the first time.

Fire tore through Ruby's body, scorching every nerve with its heat, taking their connection from pleasant and hesitant to full-on sizzling, with the smells of the beach and the flavours of their lunch in each breath and taste.

Kern's groan echoed her own as their kiss deepened, until nothing but the pleasure of kissing and touching each other consumed their every thought.

When they finally broke apart, breath ragged, bodies close and smouldering, Ruby opened her eyes and stared at Kern with awe. 'I think I rather liked that.'

Kern grinned and pulled her close again. 'Yeah, me too.'

Kern climbed over the fence that ran along the east side of MacKinley farm and walked towards a huge oak tree. Hundreds of years old, the tree had lived through several generations of his late wife's family.

Sitting down on the bench set purposely underneath the tree's vast canopy, he stared out at the darkening night, broken only by the yellow glow from a single window of the large house in the distance.

Corinne's father was probably sitting in his study, watching history programmes. They'd barely spoken at Corinne's funeral, aware that they shared a common bond neither of them wished to acknowledge. How they'd both failed to make Corinne happy.

A rustle sounded in the darkness...probably a nocturnal animal searching for food—or maybe the spirits of Corinne's family, horrified that he'd dared to trespass on the place where they scattered the remains of their family members and wanting to make their displeasure known.

The family hadn't invited him to witness Corinne's ashes being scattered. But then he'd never asked to be there. That part of his life was over. The ties finally broken so they could all move on.

'What a mess we created, Corinne,' Kern murmured aloud. 'Who'd have thought we'd both return to Dorset? Back to the homes we ran from as stupid kids, concerned only with breaking away from our families.'

An owl hooted in the darkness and the rustling in the bushes ceased.

Kern closed his eyes and continued with his one-sided conversation. 'I never was enough for you, was I? I tried to be, but we both know I wasn't. I loved you for so many years...but perhaps if we'd divorced you'd have found happiness with someone else. Someone who understood you better than I did. Someone whose opinion you would listen to and not resent. Someone capable of giving you a child, or at least easing your pain over the absence of one. I didn't know how to heal that ache you carried inside.'

He tilted his head and stared up at the few stars already showing in the sky.

'Don't you think I ached for a child too? I wanted to adopt, but you always refused to consider it.' He shook his head. 'I guess we were both guilty of never facing things head-on. Of not having that one important conversation. I tried a few times...but when I saw the pain in your eyes I gave up. I used work as an excuse to ignore your unhappiness, and you refused to face the reality of never becoming a mother. I hate it that after all our years together we just grew apart.'

He stopped and swallowed the lump in his throat that the memory caused.

'Do you still hate me? That last morning when I suggested you go and talk to the doctor, you yelled at me that you did. Do you hate me all the way from heaven?'

He closed his eyes and shifted forward on the bench.

'If I had the power to change the last few years, I would. But things were never going to change when you didn't want them to. I think deep down you just didn't know how to take those steps. Steps you had to take alone, to really find peace inside your heart. The only thing your father said to me at the funeral was that a person can only be helped when their troubled soul desires it. And it's taken me a long time to realise he's right. No doctor or counsellor in the world was going to reach you unless you decided to listen.'

He rubbed a hand over his forehead before he continued.

'You left me with nothing, Corinne. I lost it all. The yard, the horses, respect—even the desire to succeed. You finally achieved the revenge you wanted. I sold the trophies and I watched the yard being sold to a man I couldn't stand. Lost our home because I had debts to clear and no other way to pay them. You accused me of not listening to you that last morning, and then you made damn sure I had no choice but to.'

He leaned back again.

'I suppose you want to know why I've come home when I always swore never to? Well, I said it right there. It's home. And when things are rough that's where you need to be.'

He stood up and shoved his hands into his jean pockets.

'Jacob's offered me a job, but Eloise wants me to stay and start over. Why didn't you tell me she'd called several times over the years? Secrets and disappointments are what we became, Corinne, didn't we?'

His thoughts returned to that afternoon at the beach and Ruby. Even now, hours later, he could still taste her sweet kisses. She was an angel who deserved a man with means and drive. Not an undecided 'has-been' stuck at rock-bottom, unsure how to take the first step to something better. Not a man with lingering connections to a world that had once caused her great pain regardless of her reassurances.

A decent man would walk away from Ruby and the promise of what could be. Trouble was, after kissing her the last thing Kern desired was to be decent.

'I'll always regret the mistakes we made,' he

whispered into the darkness. 'But I swear I've learnt from them. I hope someone in the next life can make you happy. As for me—well, I think it's time I made up my mind about the future, don't you?'

CHAPTER ELEVEN

RUBY RESTED HER hands on the cardboard box and eyed the small red-haired boy standing on the opposite side of the examination table with caution. 'So, Jack, who's inside here?'

The nine-year-old stared at her, suspicion twinkling in his grey eyes. He wiped a hand across his nose and sniffed. 'Roger.'

'Roger?' she repeated.

Roger the rat? Roger the snake? Roger the tarantula? Or Roger the boy's baby brother?

Anne had mentioned that Jack liked to play jokes on people. Did he consider the new vet an easy target?

'And who is Roger?' she asked, hoping for a hint of what lurked inside the box.

'He's my best friend,' Jack declared, giving his runny nose another wipe.

Ruby resisted the urge to fetch a tissue from the box on the desk behind her and insist he blow it. Instead, she asked, 'And what species is Roger?'

The boy frowned. 'What?'

'I mean what type of animal is Roger? Am I likely to get my fingers bitten if I wiggle them inside?'

Jack's mum chuckled from the chair in the corner.

'You may do,' Jack said, and then clearly recalled the first part of her question. 'He's a guinea pig. *My* guinea pig. And he's two years old.'

'Not a vet-eating monster, then?' she quizzed, flashing the boy a grin.

Jack laughed. 'Cool!'

For a spectator, perhaps, but Ruby preferred to keep her fingers and the rest of her body in one piece, safe from unidentified creatures lurking inside cardboard boxes.

'What's wrong with Roger?' Ruby kept her hands on the box, not in a hurry to investigate further until she had more information. Naturally nervous creatures, guinea pigs were best left alone until she'd discovered the problem.

'His teeth are too long,' Jack said. 'He can't eat all his food.'

It was a common issue with guinea pigs.

Ruby softly tapped the box's top flaps. 'I see... And is it just Roger in here?'

'Yes.'

'Okay. Well, I think to make Roger happier I'm going to dim the overhead light for a moment. He's been cooped up in the darkness, so we don't want to startle him with a bright light, do we?'

Jack stayed silent while she took care of the light. Returning to the table, she opened the box and peered inside, to find a brown and white guinea pig twitching its nose and staring at her.

'Hey, Roger,' she murmured softly. 'How are you doing?'

Lifting the guinea pig out, she supported its weight in one palm and carefully checked over its mouth. Yes, those teeth definitely needed some dental work. Far too big for comfortable eating.

'Well, Jack, you are absolutely right. Roger's front teeth are way too big, and they need filing so he can eat with ease.'

'Will it make them smaller?' Jack asked,

reaching out to stroke a dirty finger over his pet's tummy.

'Yes—and I think it might be best for Roger to come back and stay with us for a morning, so we can check his other teeth. Sometimes they grow too big as well, and can make a guinea pig's tongue sore. Let's go and make an appointment with Anne.'

Together, with Roger back in his box, they headed to Reception and quickly made an appointment for Roger to return the next day.

Back in the consultation room, Ruby had turned her attention to clearing up when May, one of the practice nurses, knocked on the door.

'There's a man in Reception asking to speak with you.'

'A man?' Ruby asked. 'Did he give a name?'

'Yeah, Kern MacKinley. Shall I send him in? You've ten minutes before your next appointment. And Mrs Flutter and her Dobermans are always late.'

Ruby nodded. Perhaps he had a problem with Evie? Or wanted to rearrange their dinner date? Maybe share more of his wonderful kisses?

Just the thought set off fizzles of delight inside her stomach. She liked kissing Kern very much. In fact, she struggled not to think about his lips and his mouth and how they'd sent her skin tingling and warmed all her intimate parts...

Shaking some sense into herself, she quickly rinsed her hands under the tap. Drying them with a paper towel, she tried to steady her breathing as she waited for the man who occupied her thoughts to walk in.

'Hi,' Kern greeted her when he strolled into the room moments later, filling the spacious area with his charisma. The black jumper he wore brought out the blue of his eyes, sending those fizzles into manic spins.

'What's wrong?' she asked, shoving her hands into her white lab coat's pockets.

He chuckled and stepped further into the room. 'Now, why do you think there's something wrong?'

She wrinkled her nose. 'Because you mostly search me out when you want a favour,' she pointed out.

He slapped a hand to his chest in mock pain. 'There you go again—hurting my male pride with your cruel but unfortunately true observations.' He shook his head. 'And it really is true, isn't it?'

She nodded. 'Yep.'

'But what you *haven't* realised is that although I may want something from you—normally your expertise—I always give back in return.'

She snorted. 'Really?'

'Yes,' he insisted. 'The night you tended Evie, I gave you a piggyback.'

She folded her arms and leaned against the cupboards behind her. 'Yes, you did. How silly of me to forget.'

'And when we travelled to check out the horse, I provided a meal—'

'Your aunt did,' she corrected. 'She made all the food.'

'Only because I don't have use of a kitchen,' he said smoothly.

She shook her head and demanded, 'Okay MacKinley, what are you after this time?'

He grinned. 'Your professional skills.'

'Again?' she huffed. 'You *do* realise there's more to me than my job, don't you?'

He let his eyes slowly run over her, visually caressing each and every curve of her body.

'Oh, believe me, Ruby... I am more than conscious of that fact.'

Blushing, she straightened. 'Which horse
needs my help this time?'

'I suspect Mabel Star has a blocked tear duct.
She has gunk weeping from her left eye.'

Ruby nodded, mindful that her next patient
must have arrived. 'Okay, I'll pop in on my way
home from work and take a look.'

'Thank you.'

She called out to him as he turned to leave.
'My favours come with a price, MacKinley.'

He glanced back with a strange, almost sad
expression on his face. 'I know that, Ruby. Believe me, I know...'

Ruby parked her car on the dirt track outside
the MacKinley stables, smiling when she spotted Kern strolling out to meet her. The man's
easy saunter always made her stop and take a
breath—his loose movements were a sight to
relish.

'Hey,' he said, opening her door. 'Thanks for
stopping by.'

Ruby slipped out, her heart-rate skipping as
she straightened up in the small space between

the man and the car. A space Kern appeared in no rush to widen.

'No problem. You suspect a blocked tear duct?'

'Yeah,' Kern said, finally stepping away. 'The discharge from her eye has increased since this morning.'

Ruby grabbed her medical case from the back seat. 'I have everything here to flush out any blockage—except an assistant to help me.'

Kern slipped her case from her hold before she could argue and offered, 'I work well under instruction. Will I do?'

She scoffed and followed him towards the stables. 'Not from what I've seen, MacKinley. I'd say you're a rebel at heart.'

She followed him through the entrance, her eyes flicking to his very nice backside, encased in the usual worn jeans. His blue-and-white-checked shirt sat half untucked at the waistband. Ruby's fingers itched to explore beneath the material. To lift the fabric and slide her hands inside over his warm flesh.

The trouble was his remarks earlier, as he'd left the practice, concerned her.

Was he still struggling with his conscience?

Concerned that it was too soon after he'd lost his wife? Worried that people might judge him for moving on? That he owed his wife a decent mourning period even though it seemed their marriage, by Kern's own statements, hadn't included any closeness towards the end. Did the chemistry between them distress him? Or did the difference in age really matter to him?

Friends didn't kiss passionately. So what were they? Not friends with benefits. Surely he didn't see them as such a thing? She wished she knew how he felt, because then she might begin to understand her own feelings.

Did he worry that she wanted more than just kisses?

Did she want more?

Ruby's gaze moved over the man once again, taking in every inch of his firm body and wide shoulders. Yes, she did—and not only physically. She craved Kern's company when they were apart. She dreamt about him at night. She desired his kisses and wanted the right to take one whenever the urge came over her.

She wanted Kern MacKinley. Every single bit of him. And that fact scared her and excited her.

She yearned for the right to pull him close

and run her tongue along the curve of his neck. To tug his shirt apart, flick the buttons who cared where and scatter kisses over his chest and stomach.

'Ruby?'

Blinking, she dragged herself from her luscious wondering. 'If you can lead Mabel Star out here into the aisle, where there's more room to examine her, that would be wonderful.'

'Of course.'

She was aware that the procedure for clearing a horse's blocked tear duct could be challenging. 'Most horses hate having the flush done,' she told him. 'She might fidget quite a bit.'

Kern nodded and headed to the rear of the stables to fetch the mare. Ruby sorted through her equipment, pushing all unanswered questions and queries from her mind. Pondering over what Kern thought and indulging in scrumptious fantasies would have to wait. Right now, Mabel Star required all her attention.

When the comforting and familiar clip-clop of hoofs on concrete sounded in the aisle, Ruby turned and waited for man and horse to reach her before she slowly approached the mare.

Examining the left eye, she studied the crusty

discharge weeping heavily from the corner. 'Okay, it's probably an obstruction. She hasn't hit her nose recently?'

'Not that I've seen.'

Ruby nodded. 'First I'll flood the eye with fluorescein dye. After five minutes we'll have a clearer idea as to what's going on.'

Kern nodded, and continued to hold Mabel Star while Ruby fetched the dye and applied it. After a few minutes, when hardly any dye had dripped out of the mare's nose, it was obvious the problem was down to a blockage.

'Right, I suggest we sedate Mabel Star, and then place a tube inside the tear duct at the nostril end and flush it out with saline. That should remove any build-up that's inside.'

She stopped when footsteps sounded behind her and Kern's friend Jacob walked through the entrance.

Kern remained holding Mabel Star, but nodded to his friend. 'Back already? Anyone would think you like it here. Two visits in a week?'

Jacob grinned. 'Yeah... Had a call from a friend in Ireland. Thought that as I was passing on the way to the airport I'd pop in and see if you've thought any more about that job offer.'

'I'm considering it,' Kern said, though most of his attention stayed on Mabel Star. 'I've called the man and set up a meeting.'

'Good.' Jacob indicated the horse. 'Problem?'

'Blocked tear duct. Nothing Ruby can't fix.'

Warmed by his faith in her ability, Ruby sedated Mabel Star and gathered everything she needed. Flushing out a horse's tear duct was tricky, especially if the horse resented the intrusion of the tube inserted into the tear duct. And horses always did. Though she didn't blame them. Having something shoved into her nose by a stranger would hardly impress Ruby, either.

Laying a gentle hand on the mare's face, she did her best to reassure the old girl, conscious of Jacob and Kern close by.

Kern nodded at his friend. 'Safe journey. Stay in the saddle and in your own bed.'

Jacob laughed. 'I'll do my best. Seriously, keep thinking about the offer. It's a good one. And give me first dibs on riding your next champion.'

'I will,' Kern promised, glancing Ruby's way.

Jacob nodded to Ruby before leaving the building.

Ruby waited for the sound of Jacob's car being driven away before she asked, 'Your friend has offered you a job?'

'Yes,' Kern confirmed. 'He has connections with someone who's eager for me to manage a yard for him. I've agreed to meet with him— that's all.'

Ruby heart skipped. Neither Kern's bland expression nor his tone gave away his feelings concerning the offer. Did it intrigue him enough to make him consider leaving Dorset?

'Sounds interesting,' she said.

Kern frowned. 'Do you think so?'

She shrugged, only interested in what *he* thought. 'What do *you* think?'

'If I was young and starting off in the game again, I might consider it. But I'm not used to answering to anyone except the odd owner who hasn't learnt to trust my opinion.'

Ruby gathered a thin tube and a syringe filled with saline. 'She may pull and fuss while we do this,' she warned.

'I have her.'

Kern soothed Mabel Star, holding her head firmly. He stroked the mare's ear as Ruby fed the tube into the small tear duct situated inside the nose. Mabel Star tugged for a moment, but settled long enough for Ruby to squirt the fluid inside. Seconds later a mixture of fluorescein dye and saline fluid gushed out of her eye.

'But you've agreed to think about it?' asked Ruby.

Kern soothed Mabel Star again as she tugged and stepped backwards.

Confident the procedure had removed any blockage, Ruby swapped sides and repeated the process in the mare's other nostril. Within minutes both sides were washed out.

'Yes,' said Kern.

Ruby retrieved a wad of sterile tissue from her bag and mopped away the mess around Mabel Star's eyes. 'I suppose it is a way to return to racing...'

Kern snorted. 'At the beck and call of a rich man who could cut me loose any time he chooses to? What if I went to work for him and then in a year's time he decided to pack it in and invest in racing cars instead? I'd be cast aside and left in the dirt. Same for any staff who worked for me. I've seen it happen before.'

'Yet you're still considering it?' she guessed,

sensing his indecision, despite his reservations. 'You must miss racing...'

Kern didn't answer straight away, but when he did, he shrugged. 'What else am I going to do, Ruby? As Eloise once pointed out, I know nothing else. My whole life has revolved around horses. From the time I sat on one to the day I lifted my last winner's cup I've lived and breathed racing. And it's not just about the winning. It's the people, the smells, the kick of seeing a horse you've trained from a youngster and watched improve cross the winner's line to the roar of the crowd. The relief when it's comes home safe and well.'

She stared at the flickering emotions crossing his face as he spoke. A large part of her understood his words. She'd seen the same love for the sport in her father's expression years before.

'You love it,' she said.

Kern nodded. 'I do. But there's a flipside to everything I've mentioned. If I start out on my own again, it will require a lot of work and time—God knows this land needs a small miracle to get it to a half-decent standard.'

'But it would be yours,' she reminded him, confident he could achieve it.

'Yes,' he agreed. 'As well as all the debts and the bills. And all the headaches running a yard involves. Plus the added problem of Fin.'

'You've done it before.'

His eyes met hers. 'What do you think I should do?'

She pondered the question for a moment. Not sure how to advise him. Every career suffered highs and lows. He'd experienced both. 'I think you should consider what you really want deep in your heart. You're in a better position this time because you've done it once and understand what's required.'

'I've also lost everything,' he said ruefully.

Ruby stroked a hand down Mabel Star's face. 'Your wife was sick, Kern. You need to forgive what she did.'

'I do forgive her.' He smiled softly. 'I always forgave her. I think maybe that was the problem. I was weak.'

'For loving someone so deeply? Isn't that what real love is? Not simply the sweet, loving times, but the rough moments too? From what you've told me, you saw your wife as your friend too. And a good friend doesn't let go when things get tough. A friend grips on—even if it's hard, and perhaps the love changes and ebbs—a friend cares enough to shelter a person when they need it. I think Corinne trusted you to do so…trusted you to be her safety. I doubt she meant to do what she did. I think perhaps it's like you said. She hit her final place where everything became too much.'

'So wise…' Kern murmured.

'Your aunt once said we survive trauma and move on. Let Corinne go and do the same. I think it's time.'

'Maybe…' he said. 'I'll put Mabel Star in her stable.'

Ruby reached out and stopped him. 'When do you meet with this man?'

He let out a long sigh. 'The morning of the parade. I figure I've nothing to lose by listening to him. What is there to keep me here? A derelict stable? Weed-thick land?'

Me, Ruby whispered in her heart. *I'm here if you'd open your blinkered eyes and see how much I care for you.*

'So our kisses meant nothing to you?' The question escaped and hung between them. Flushing, she turned away. 'Sorry. I didn't mean to ask that.'

Kern reached for her. 'Ruby, I—'

'Don't!' she snapped, suddenly fed up with his indecision. 'Don't stand there and lie to me. If they were just a way to pass the time, then have the guts to say so. I'm a woman, not a child. I can take the truth.'

'Of course they weren't. I told you there's a strong connection—'

'But not strong enough for you to consider taking it further than kisses,' she guessed, suddenly feeling foolish. She sounded like a teenager, whining because a hot boy wished to dump her.

But she couldn't help feeling used by Kern. One minute she'd believed they were friends and the next they'd been kissing, making her think he wanted to take their relationship further. But now he was talking about leaving and the knowledge hurt. Really hurt.

'Look, it's okay,' she insisted. 'If I was just a bit of fun—'

'Don't you dare insult either of us with that comment. The truth is I desire you. I want to take you to bed right now and love you hard. I ache to kiss every inch of your soft skin. Taste you until I crave no other flavour in my mouth.

But I daren't. Because I fail people. I failed
Corinne, I failed the owners of the horses who
put their trust in me, and I failed my family
when I stayed away.'

'You didn't fail—'

'I did. But I swear to God I am not going to
fail you. I'm not going to see your respect and
affection die because of what I fail to do. Yes,
I want to hold you and kiss you, but I won't—
because what I feel here in my heart is more
than I have ever felt for anyone else. We could
never be just friends, Ruby, because I'd always
yearn for more. And if we took it further and it
all went wrong it would break my heart completely.'

'But what if I want to take the risk?' she
asked. 'Don't you care about what *I* want?'

'I refuse to let you take the risk.'

'Coward!' she spat, furious that he thought
he could make that decision on her behalf.

'What did you call me?'

'A coward!' she repeated. 'You stand there,
all proud and virtuous. Spouting declarations
of how you're doing it to protect me. The truth
is you're doing it to protect yourself. Because
you're a coward, too scared to take a chance.'

'You don't understand—'

'Don't patronise me!' she yelled. 'I understand that you won't give us a chance of a relationship because you're scared. I get that. I was scared for years until I came to Dorset and met you. You've helped me to see that being scared of life is no real life. You've shown me how much I've been missing out on.'

'Ruby—'

'I'm not Corinne. Any relationship we have will be ours. It will be different. Because I'm a different person. You cannot judge any future relationship with the same eyes as you did your marriage. Everyone is unique.'

'I know.'

'So don't use your marriage as an excuse to conceal your fear. If you want to take this job, then go. If you want to stay—fine. But don't bother me unless you meant those kisses and you want to build on them. It takes courage to pick up and start living again. Just make a decision and get on with it.'

Grabbing her belongings together, she rushed from the stables, ignoring the pain in her chest and the overwhelming urge to cry.

'Ruby!'

Forcing herself to keep going, she jumped in her car and drove away. If Kern didn't want a relationship, then it was his loss. Any man she let inside her heart would be there because he wanted her more than anything else in life. If Kern didn't feel that, then it was better to let him go.

CHAPTER TWELVE

RUBY SWIPED THE wet flannel over her face and stared at her reflection in the bathroom mirror. For the first time in weeks, months, or maybe even years, she studied her uncovered features with a critical focus she normally avoided.

Without the make-up she wore throughout the day she could witness her real self. Not the person she showed the world, but the person beneath the concealer, beneath the past's heavy veneer and her parents' scandal. The adult version of the sixteen-year-old who'd discovered that few people around her were trustworthy.

Usually her brain instantly connected her own face with her mother's image, but today, staring at her reflection, she saw herself. She wasn't the child disappointed by her parents and then left alone by one's abandonment and the other's grief. She was a grown woman who'd worked hard to achieve the career she wanted and the life she loved.

When Kern had asked that day on the beach who the real Ruby Day was she'd had no answer. She'd run for so long, wanting to forget the beginning of her life, ashamed and hurt by her parents' actions. Back then, she'd craved normality and peace, but somehow over the years she'd forgotten that she deserved to be herself too.

Leaning forward, she stared harder at her reflection. Seeing her cat's eyes free of black eyeliner and the too-plump mouth. Grabbing a handful of her black curls, she laughed at the image. She didn't resemble her mother at all. She actually looked like herself. Why had she never seen that before?

She was exhausted after years of playing a part and putting on a front. She wanted to roll out of bed and be Ruby. She didn't want to wear make-up all the time. She wanted to let her skin breathe, to undo all the wrappings she'd wound round and round herself, convinced they were protecting her from hurt.

But they hadn't protected her. Instead, they'd suppressed her and hidden away her real self. Suffocating her until she could barely breathe.

And then Kern had come along and gently

teased her into wanting to unravel those layers inch by inch, until her head spun and her heart raced and she felt free for the first time in years.

As a grown woman she could cope with life and what the future threw her way without the need for armour of any kind. It was time to be the person deep inside her heart and march into the future as the strong, capable woman she was.

She couldn't accuse Kern of being cowardly and then continue to be the same herself.

Picking up her eyeliner, she swiped a line under her lower lashes and then stepped away. No concealer, no eyeshadow and no lipstick. Just eyeliner and her silver lip ring. She didn't require anything more.

Today, for the first time since the age of sixteen, the real Ruby Day was coming out to play. And she couldn't wait to show herself off to the world.

Leaving the bathroom, Ruby headed to the bedroom. Dog was stretched out on his own large bed for a change, snoring. She grinned and stroked a hand over his chest, her heart full of love for her sweet boy.

Opening the wardrobe door, she withdrew the white lace Victorian dress she'd found online—original, with little wear. She ran her hand over the superb detailed lacework, wondering about the woman who'd first worn it. Had that mystery lady's heart thumped with excitement and fear as she'd prepared to dress all those years ago?

Slipping the dress off the hanger, she pulled it on, quickly fixing the miniature buttons and ribbon ties around the high lace neck. Lace sleeves had buttoned cuffs, and a matching lace frill draped into a point at the front. The dress fitted perfectly, and for the first time in years Ruby felt feminine in a totally different way.

'What do you think, Dog? Will Kern like me dressed like this? Will he still be talking to me after the way I behaved the other day?'

Lifting a large white hat, she placed it on her head and pinned it with the long hat pin she'd bought from an antique shop. No longer Ruby the Goth. Today she'd be Ruby the Victorian. And tomorrow she'd start living her life simply as Ruby Day, the local vet who could heal animals with her hands.

The violent fluttering in her stomach intensified and she laughed once again. Yes, it was definitely time to be the authentic Ruby—and amazingly, she couldn't wait.

'Ruby you look beautiful!' Kiki rushed over and wrapped Ruby in a hug. 'Utterly charming. I love the dress.'

'Let go,' Alex ordered his wife, sending Ruby an apologetic glance as they joined her and Eloise in a local field with all the other parade participants.

The town had gone full Victorian, and everyone wore outfits suitable for extras in a Dickens adaptation. Several food and beer tents were pitched close by, and a couple of steamrollers puffed and smoked on the other side of the field. A couple of cows complained as their owners pulled them across the grass, and horses waited patiently beside farm wagons and carts.

In the middle of the crowded field was a wagon decorated with a giant papier mâché chicken, which Eloise had informed Ruby was a replica of one pictured in a Dorset newspaper from the 1800s. It shifted precariously, despite its rope fastenings.

'I'm only hugging her,' Kiki insisted, continuing to push the air out of Ruby's lungs.

Alex gently detached his wife. 'No, you're scaring her. Though it would make a nice change for a member of staff to leave because of *your* irrational behaviour instead of mine.'

Panic entered Kiki's gaze. 'Ruby's not going to leave—are you? Please don't. You can have a partnership in the business if you promise to stay. Just say yes.'

'I—I…' She glanced at her boss for help.

'Early stages of pregnancy,' Alex explained, groaning as his wife suddenly rushed off to hug a passing old man. 'She can't keep her hands to herself.'

'Where is MacKinley?'

Ruby glanced around the crowded field, filled with town folk eager to be part of this yearly tradition. 'I don't know. He should be here by now.'

Alex studied her outfit with a deep frown. 'You do look lovely—but you're not giving up the Goth look for good, are you?'

Smiling shyly, she reassured her boss. 'No. But I feel it's time for a change. It's quite nice to wear white instead of black.'

Alex regarded her for a moment before he nodded. 'Good, because you should never change yourself for anyone, Ruby. Anyone decent will want you for yourself—otherwise they don't deserve you.'

Touched by his words and obvious concern, she shook her head. 'I'm not doing it for anyone. I'm doing it for me. Thanks again for understanding yesterday.'

After she'd finished the previous day's consultations Ruby had sought Alex out and explained everything to him. She had told him about her ability to heal animals and who her parents had been. Having recently confessed everything to Kern, telling her boss had come more easily than she'd imagined. And doing so had felt right.

After he'd listened, Alex had leaned back in his chair and asked if she'd be willing to treat some clients for whom traditional drugs weren't helping or working. He'd explained how he wanted to develop the holistic side of their treatments and offer owners a varied choice for their pets and animals.

'You're gifted,' Alex said. 'I'd be a fool not to encourage you to use your talent.' With a wave goodbye, he'd added, 'Be proud of your gift, Ruby. It's an important part of who you are. And maybe we can discuss the idea of partnership in a year or so. With another baby on the way, I'd like to spend more time at home with my family.'

Now Ruby smiled, her affection for her boss growing. Alex Morsi was a very nice man. Professor Handel deserved a large bunch of flowers for insisting that Ruby travel to 'one last interview'. Coming to Dorset had changed not only her fortune, but her life.

'Where's Kern?' Eloise demanded, interrupting Ruby's thoughts.

She'd finished harnessing Mabel Star and putting her to the cart. The sweet mare looked glorious with her plaited mane and shiny coat.

Feeling uneasy, Ruby shrugged. 'I don't know.'

She checked her phone again, but there were still no messages from Kern or anyone else. For the umpteenth time she wondered how his meeting had gone. Had the man persuaded Kern to become his trainer? Had Kern seized the opportunity to go back into the work he loved? Had money influenced his decision? Or the way she'd shouted at him and told him to make up his mind? Did he resent her interference in his life?

'He had a meeting in town this morning,' Ruby said. 'Perhaps he's been delayed, or has stopped to pick up supplies for the horses?'

'What meeting?' Eloise demanded, her eyes narrowing on Ruby.

Ruby sighed, wishing she'd kept quiet. It was one thing for her to worry, but Eloise deserved to hear about the job offer from her nephew. 'I'm not sure...'

'Don't lie,' Eloise scolded. 'You're terrible at it and your face gives you away. Come on—tell me what this meeting was for.'

'A friend of his recently sought him out and offered him the chance of a job training horses for some rich man. Kern told me that he had agreed to meet the man this morning, but that's all he said.'

'I hope he hasn't left without telling anyone,' Eloise said, fiddling with her necklace.

Ruby had noted that she did so whenever she was worried or concerned.

'It's what he did before.'

'He was young then,' Ruby pointed out, not

wanting to contemplate the notion of Kern having gone without saying goodbye. 'I'm sure he'd talk to you first. Maybe he can't get through the traffic outside of town. The roads are busy.'

'I hope so,' Eloise muttered, patting Mabel Star.

Darkness crept into Ruby's heart at Eloise's concern. The horrible suspicion that Kern might have chosen to sneak away refused to stay quiet. Surely he wouldn't hurt his aunt again? He had responsibilities both to his elderly relative and MacKinley farm.

But what if this man Kern had met had managed to talk him into leaving and insisted he do so immediately? How long did it take to set up a yard, anyway? Would Kern prefer to go without saying goodbye to her? Did the time they spent together, getting to know each other, mean nothing to him? She knew he wanted her, but was he determined to deny them both?

'Come on.' Eloise sighed. 'If Kern doesn't arrive soon, I'll drive the cart in the parade.'

Giving Eloise's arm a reassuring rub, Ruby said, 'At least you *can* drive it. We'd be in real trouble if I had to do it.'

Eloise paled and admitted, 'To be honest, I

struggled to get the hang of it years ago, but I'm sure we'll manage.'

'There's still half an hour until we're due to leave,' Ruby soothed, glancing towards the entrance to the field. 'I'm sure Kern will arrive soon.'

The old woman nodded, unable to hide the tears in her eyes. 'I'm afraid my nephew may have decided not to come. Goodbyes always were a problem for him.'

'Come on. Don't do this to me.'

Kern stared at his phone, silently praying for it to come to life, despite knowing it was a wasted hope. The thing was deader than a medieval skeleton.

His meeting in town that morning with the Sheikh had cemented the decision he'd reached the night Ruby had walked out. After a phone call to one of the men who'd helped him months before, he'd spent the rest of his time making plans. Plans necessary to rebuild his life.

Everything was in place except for one thing. Ruby. The woman he'd been desperately trying to get hold of since leaving the local auction house after dropping off some of his parents' old furniture and belongings. Not precious stuff, but hopefully decent enough to raise enough funds to cover the next six months' bills and expenses.

Shoving the phone into the pocket of his black trousers, he tugged at the blue neck scarf around his throat. With the sleeves of his white shirt rolled up, his traditional Victorian farmer's garb was completed with a plain brown waistcoat.

Already running late, he had no time to linger. Ruby, his partner for the parade, would be waiting. The other half of the Victorian courting couple they were playing.

Only it didn't feel like playing to him. His mind was clear for the first time in months.

When Ruby had called him a coward, he'd balked at the criticism. But once his ego had shifted out of the way he'd faced the ugly truth. A truth she'd told him straight. Denying his desire for her *was* cowardly—and unbelievably stupid when he knew how precious life and happiness was.

With a glance over at Evie, he led the filly outside into the yard. 'How do you fancy a run, girl? I need your help. Don't get jealous, but there's a woman I want to impress and I just hope I can talk her into listening.'

'Where's Ruby?' Kern led Evie over to where Alex Morsi and his wife stood, eating ice creams. Their baby girl gurgled from her pram, looking as though she'd been in a fight with an ice cream monster.

'Where have you been?' Kiki demanded, scooping ice cream onto a small wooden stick.

'I got stuck in town and my phone died when I reached home,' Kern explained.

'She's gone,' Alex said, nodding to the country road going west into town. 'Left about ten minutes ago.'

Kern's stomach dipped and panic swirled through his chest. Gone? Had Ruby decided to leave Dorset after their argument? Surely she'd stay for her job at the practice?

He swallowed hard, and asked, 'Gone?'

Alex nodded. 'The organisers ordered them to line up for the parade. If you listen, you can hear the band playing.'

Kern stomach turned over as another thought hit him. 'Who's driving the cart?'

The other two stared at him, before answering together, 'Eloise.'

The sickening twist inside his body became full-on dread. 'I need to stop them.'

'Why?' Alex asked, following him as he turned to his horse.

Kern mounted Evie again and turned the filly towards the gated entrance. 'Last time Eloise drove a cart she ended up in a bush. Unless she's had lessons since I've been gone, there's every chance they'll have an accident.'

'You'd better hurry!' Alex yelled. 'I don't want to search for another vet. Ruby has talents barely explored.'

Kern grinned at the man's words. Ruby did indeed have talents, and he intended for her to use every single one. That was if she forgave him for his stupidity and gave him another chance.

Riding through the gate, Kern headed in the direction of town. Small groups of people wandered along the pavements. The red, white and blue bunting and flags strung on lamps and gateposts fluttered in the slight breeze.

Up ahead, he caught sight of a vintage tractor, hissing out smoke as it rolled along. Carefully, he eased Evie over to the right-hand side of the road, glad the town council had closed it to traffic. After passing a wagon loaded with children dressed in white pinafores and flat caps, he finally spotted the cart.

Riding along at the driver's side, he called out, 'Taking over my job, Aunt Eloise?'

Eloise sighed heavily. 'Thank goodness. I can't stop shaking—and I'm sure poor Mabel Star can feel it.'

'Pull over in the next lay-by and we'll swap transport.'

Within minutes they'd stopped, and Eloise climbed down from the cart and happily took Evie's reins from her nephew. 'I'll walk Evie back and meet you two at the field after the parade.'

Ruby turned to Kern as he climbed into the cart and reached for the reins. 'I thought you'd taken the job and left.'

Kern grasped her hand and squeezed it. 'Let's do the parade and then I've important news to tell you.'

'Will I like it?' she asked.

'I'm not sure,' he admitted, suddenly nervous. What if Ruby hated his decision? What if she decided she only wanted him as a friend and nothing else? How could he show her that he was ready to be brave?

With a flare of determination, Kern flicked the reins. Ruby might have doubts, but he was damned if he was going to let her go without fighting to prove to her that if she took a chance on him he'd never fail again.

Ruby's heart thudded harder than the town's brass band's drum as Kern drove the cart away from the crowds and through the countryside. The parade was over, and everyone involved was slowly making their way back to the field to spend the rest of the afternoon relaxing and enjoying refreshment.

Gripping her hands together on her lap, she glanced at Kern and asked, 'Where are we going?'

Kern took a deep breath, before asking, 'Did you really think I'd leave without speaking to you again? Without saying goodbye? I'm disappointed, Ruby.'

'I didn't know what to think,' she admitted. 'The job offer sounded good, and after our discussion I thought—'

'It wasn't a discussion,' he corrected. 'It was our first fight.'

'Oh,' she said. 'Does that mean there are going to be more?'

He chuckled and slid a glance her way. 'I hope so. You're right—the job is a great opportunity for someone. I won't lie to you, I did consider it for a moment. But then we went to the beach and I knew deep in my soul I wasn't going anywhere. Dorset is home. I've missed it and been away from it for too long. This is where I'm going to start over. It's time to get back to work. I owe it to my family. Especially to my mother, who must be cursing from heaven at my endless wavering.'

'You've finally decided?'

He nodded. 'It's time I restored MacKinley farm and the family name. Make the old place a home again. A home filled with a ton of love. Just like it used to be.'

Ruby licked her lips, her heart swelling with hope. 'Sounds like a wonderful idea.'

Kern turned off the country lane into a familiar drive and stopped the cart once they were outside his childhood home. Ruby glanced at the old run-down farmhouse.

Wrapping the reins around the brake, Kern twisted on the seat and stared at her. 'I want to spend time with my aunt and with the sweet, wonderful woman I'm starting to care about. That's if you'll give me a chance?'

Ruby eyes widened. 'Me?'

'Who else?' he asked. 'Ruby, I am everything you shouldn't want, but I'm hoping you'll give us a go anyway. I'm asking for a chance to show you how good we can be. I want to make you happy, Ruby. I want to prove to you that I'm no coward when it comes to our love.'

'Are you sure this is what you truly want—?'

Kern brushed her knuckles with a kiss. 'You're all I want, Ruby. You're the dream I've lived through every night since we met. When I'm with you anything seems possible. You're funny, shy and adorable. I want to spend every day around you, enjoying your company. Since that first day, when you drove onto the farm and ordered me to get dressed, something has happened to my heart.'

'What?'

He smiled and squeezed her fingers. 'It's come back to life. *You* did that. You revived me—brought me out of the coma I'd lived in for so long. If you want to leave and run, then fine—pack your caravan and drive away. But every time you glance in the rear-view mirror you'll see me, coming right after you.'

Ruby grinned. 'Will that be on horseback or in a cart?'

'I'll follow you until you're ready to build a life with me. A better one for both of us. Let me give you a home. Somewhere safe and permanent. Somewhere we can stay for ever. Where you can make long-term friends and find clients.'

'What about Fin? If you intend living on the farm, you'll need to reach a truce.'

'Fin's left and he isn't coming back. I received a solicitor's letter this morning, informing me that he has booked himself into a clinic to get help with his drinking and his depression. The accident with Dog made him realise he needed to change.'

Concern for the elderly man filled Ruby. 'Really?'

'He's also signed over his share of the farm to me. All of this—the land and the house— are mine now. All I need is for you to agree to share it with me.'

'You really mean it, don't you?' she asked, amazed by the love she saw shining from his eyes. 'You really want me?'

'I can't promise an easy time, and there won't be much money for a while, but I'll give you everything you need. I'll hold you in the night and love you through the day. I'll do all I can to make you happy.'

'Kern, come here,' she ordered, beckoning him with a finger.

He leaned nearer, his eyes never leaving hers. 'Yeah?' His loving smile touched her heart.

'Kiss me. We can talk more later, but right now you need to kiss me—because I've never felt so happy and I'm scared it might all fly away.'

'I can do that.'

'I know you can, Kern,' she said, filled with complete faith in the man sat next to her. The man she loved deeply.

And then he kissed her, and Ruby knew that the future looked perfect and she couldn't wait to live it with her man.

EPILOGUE

Six months later

RUBY SLIPPED OUT of the four-poster bed, tugging the top cover off with her. Wrapping it snugly around her naked body, she crossed the bedroom floor to the open door. Hazy sunlight peeked through the curtains, indicating that it was still early in the morning.

As she pulled the door fully open, something shiny on the carpet caught her eye. Pieces of small silver horseshoe-shaped confetti trialled along the hallway towards the narrow staircase. Intrigued, Ruby followed the trail, running down each step to the next, all the way to the lower floor of the farmhouse.

Over the last six months she and Kern had cleaned and stripped the house until it was a basic shell, ready for them to spend the next few years renovating, turning it back into a home—their home.

So far, they'd redecorated the main bedroom and the bathroom. Nothing fancy or expensive, but clean, bright and charming. A small start on the future they'd promised one another.

The smell of toast caused Ruby to pause at the kitchen door. Spying two uneaten slices left on a plate in the centre of the pine kitchen table, she wandered into the room and picked one up. Taking a bite, she murmured with pleasure before heading to the open back door.

Shivering as the early-morning air wrapped around her bare shoulders, she smiled softly as she spotted Kern, dressed only in his jeans, standing next to one of the newly mended paddocks, watching the six horses inside.

Crossing the grass, she stopped behind the man she loved, who over the last months had shown her how good a relationship could be. Not destructive, not bitter, but warm, loving and wonderful. Everything he'd promised and more. Because he was more than she'd believed possible.

Tenderly kissing her favourite spot between his shoulder blades, she greeted him. 'Hey, handsome.'

A deep chuckle hummed through Kern's body as she wrapped her arms around his waist. 'Morning, beautiful.'

'What's with the horseshoes?' she asked.

Kern stole the toast from her hand and took his own bite before turning to face her. Stroking his free hand over her tousled hair, he smiled lazily down at her. 'It's a treasure hunt.'

Her eyes widened. 'I love treasure hunts.'

'I know you do. Somewhere on me there is a gift just for you.'

She frowned and stepped back, running her eyes over his stomach up to his chest, until something dangling from the silver chain around his neck caught her attention. Something sparkly and gold.

Meeting his eyes, she whispered, 'Whose ring is that?'

He kissed her instead of answering. Long and lingering. Finally, he pulled back to speak.

'Marry me,' she butted in, before he could utter a word.

She'd barely managed to get the words out, her heart was racing so much. Shaking, she waited for his answer.

Kern glared down at her. 'That's supposed to be my line.'

She nodded and gripped the bed cover tighter to her. 'I know, but you're taking too long. Marry me.'

He pulled her back against him. 'I can't promise you a family, but I'll try to give you one. The doctors always insisted everything works as it should—perhaps you and I will get lucky.'

'We can adopt if it doesn't happen,' Ruby reassured him, aware how sensitive the subject was for him.

But she didn't need a child to be happy. As long as they woke up together each day, her heart would be full and all her needs fulfilled. She loved this man deeply. He was all she'd yearned for and prayed for in her life.

'We already have Dog and the horses.'

Kern slipped his hand into her curly hair. 'I love you.'

Her grin went from blissful to seductive. 'I love you too. Now, come back to bed and let's celebrate our engagement.'

'Are you intending to seduce me once we get there?' he asked.

She nodded, and tugged him back towards their home. 'Just make sure you do the same.'

'Oh, baby, I intend to—plus more.'

* * * * *

LET'S TALK
Romance

For exclusive extracts, competitions
and special offers, find us online:

f facebook.com/millsandboon

⬡ @millsandboonuk

🐦 @millsandboon

Or get in touch on 0844 844 1351*

For all the latest titles coming soon,
visit millsandboon.co.uk/nextmonth

*Calls cost 7p per minute plus your phone company's price per
minute access charge

Want even more
ROMANCE?

Join our bookclub today!

'Mills & Boon books, the perfect way to escape for an hour or so.'

Miss W. Dyer

'Excellent service, promptly delivered and very good subscription choices.'

Miss A. Pearson

'You get fantastic special offers and the chance to get books before they hit the shops'

Mrs V. Hall

Visit millsandbook.co.uk/Bookclub and save on brand new books.

MILLS & BOON